the secrets she kept

true crime junkies,
book seven

Christy Barritt

one
Then

SHE RAN AS FAST as she could down the dim corridor.

Sickly yellow lights buzzed overhead. The floors were scuffed and littered with leftover medical trash. The place smelled like rubbing alcohol, dust, and . . . death.

How did death smell? She should know. But she found it hard to put into words.

Gassy bodily fluids. Putrid decomposition. Metallic undertones of dried blood.

She had to get out of here.

Her legs burned.

Her lungs might explode.

Her heart beat so fast that it ached.

But she kept going.

Her life depended on it.

Despite her survival instincts, she stole a glance behind

her. The silhouette of the man lingered like a ghost trailing her.

He was still coming, still following her, still haunting.

Still striding toward her with confidence as if he knew something she didn't.

The moment reminded her of a horror movie, one where a poor hapless woman couldn't get away from the killer.

Only she was the poor, hapless woman.

And this was no movie.

A cry lodged in her throat.

This was her life. If she didn't use all her wits, she wouldn't see tomorrow.

She grabbed an old gurney and shoved it behind her, hoping it would slow the man down.

Metal clanked against the stained linoleum floor as it crashed.

"There's no need to run," the man said behind her. "There's nowhere to go. I'm going to catch you."

Another stab of fear jolted her.

No, she couldn't let him get close enough to grab her.

She scrambled around the corner, and her foot caught the edge of a cart.

She hurtled forward.

Her palms smacked against the floor, and pain lurched up her arms.

A groan escaped before she could stop it.

The footsteps were gaining speed.

The man was closing in.

Getting closer.

Closer.

Pushing aside the pain, she forced herself upright.

She had to lose him. That was her only hope.

She moved forward, arms dangling and knees like rubber.

She turned down the hallway and spotted an exit door ahead.

An exit . . .

Hope surged inside her.

If she could just get outside . . .

Using her last ounce of energy, she propelled herself forward.

She reached the door and slammed her body into it.

The door didn't budge, feeling instead like a brick wall.

Pain shot down her shoulder from the force she'd used.

"No!" Tears pressed her eyes.

She reached for the doorknob. Only . . . there wasn't one.

There wasn't even a push bar.

Terror swept through her, followed by another surge of adrenaline.

She knew exactly what that man would do to her if he caught her. Knew the kind of pain and suffering she would experience.

She threw herself against the door again and again.

Nothing happened.

It remained immovable.

She wasn't going to get this open.

The exit sign above the door glowed red, mocking her like a silent accomplice.

Using her fists, she pounded on the frigid metal. Maybe someone was outside. Someone who could help her.

Her only hope was someone being on the other side and releasing the lock for her.

She peered through the small, dusty glass panes and saw nothing but darkness.

Open-palmed, she smacked the glass. If she could just break a pane, maybe someone would hear the glass shattering.

Footsteps sounded behind her.

The man was close. So close.

Her muscles froze until she couldn't breathe.

Slowly, she turned.

Her eyes widened.

He was here.

Right behind her.

Not frazzled or out of breath.

As calm as a meadow on a breezeless day.

But his smile proved that something evil lurked beneath that peaceful exterior. Like a den of snakes beneath a field of flowers.

"You're making this much harder than it has to be," he murmured.

She pressed herself into the door, sweat spreading across her forehead. "You don't have to do this."

"Oh, but I do," he crooned.

"I won't tell anyone what you're doing. I promise I won't." Desperate promises made in a desperate attempt to stay alive.

Of *course* she would tell someone what he was doing.

He knew that. She knew that.

His smile widened. "You're right. You won't."

His hand flung up from the pocket of his lab coat. A syringe full of a milky-white liquid was tucked in his fingers, the needle already exposed.

"You're now Patient 502." Without missing a beat, he plunged it into her neck.

The prick was followed by a burning sensation.

No . . . !

She wanted to fight the effects of the medication forced into her body. But it was no use.

This was the last "normal moment" she would ever experience. She knew because she'd seen firsthand this happen before.

Her muscles became weak, and she collapsed to the floor.

When she woke up—if she woke up—her life would be a living nightmare.

two
Now

ANDI SLADE LINGERED at the corner of the building, watching the exchange in the distance.

Just what were those men up to? No good, she had no doubt about that.

As the three men walked in the opposite direction, Andi knew this was her opportunity.

She waited until they disappeared and then she darted toward the black van the two thugs had stepped out of. She knew she didn't have much time.

But she wanted to see what was inside.

If this had something to do with Victor Goodman, then there could be evidence back here.

She'd dedicated almost a year of her life to bringing this man down.

Her previous methods hadn't yielded much information.

That was why she had to take things to the next level.

She reached for the back door of the vehicle, thankful to find it unlocked. Then she climbed inside and quietly shut the door behind her.

She stared at the contents in the back of the van. Six plastic tubs with lids were stacked on top of each other in two rows. Then there were probably four different duffle bags, some fast-food wrappers, an old sweatshirt, and some rope.

Rope?

Her throat tightened.

She didn't want to think about what these men might use that for.

She needed to move quickly to see what was in these containers.

On her knees, she unzipped the largest duffle bag in the back of the van.

Her eyes widened.

Bundles of cash stared back at her. Thousands of dollars.

What were these guys up to? What was their link with Victor Goodman?

Before she could search anymore, voices sounded outside.

Her heart lurched into her throat.

Those men were back already. She thought they'd be gone longer.

She glanced at the back door. There was no time to get out.

If those guys caught her back here . . .

She swallowed hard.

She couldn't let that happen.

Quickly, she glanced around, looking for a place to hide.

There weren't many options.

She ducked behind a stack of tubs in the back of the space and pulled her knees to her chest. For once, her petite frame worked to her advantage.

She pulled a duffle bag over her feet just in case they showed. Then she held her breath and prayed those guys wouldn't open the back of the van. That they wouldn't find her.

The men continued to talk.

"I think this could be a good partnership," the third man—the one who hadn't driven up in this van—said.

"We think so too," one of the thugs said.

Then someone groaned.

Groaned?

Andi's heart sped. What was going on out there?

There was another groan. What sounded like a punch.

Then a laugh.

A cold, hard laugh.

Wait . . . they were beating this guy up, weren't they?

She heard a crash, then a clatter.

Then the front doors of the van opened, and the men climbed inside.

The engine roared to life.

She pressed her eyes shut.

Now she was *really* in trouble.

Thankfully, it was already getting dark outside. There were no windows in the back, which made the space even darker and helped conceal her presence. Maybe even helped buy her some time.

But the darkness wouldn't save her. The situation was precarious.

The two men up front began talking as the truck backed away from the warehouse and took off down the road.

Where were they going? What would Andi do when they got there?

She wasn't sure. She would have to play it by ear. Maybe she could even pretend to be a stowaway. Pretend to be homeless and looking for a place to sleep tonight.

Except she didn't look homeless, so she'd have trouble selling that one.

Her heart continued to thump in her ears.

"At least we took care of that guy back there," the driver said. "He won't be giving us any trouble."

"We have plenty of other people who could still make things difficult."

"And if they do . . . we'll do the same thing to them that we did to Max back there."

Her blood went cold.

That would include her. They would beat her to a pulp and then leave her to die.

How was she going to get out of this? She needed help, and only one person came to mind.

She carefully pulled out her phone and held it low, worried that the light from the screen might alert the men.

Then she texted Duke McAllister.

> I need your help.

She hit Send.

Only a few seconds later, he responded.

> What's up?

> I'm going to share my real-time location with you. Can you pick me up?

> Car problems?

She sent him a link to her GPS coordinates before glancing around the back of the truck as it bounced down a road. How was she supposed to respond?

Finally, she typed:

> Not exactly. Long story.

The last thing she wanted was to get into an argument with Duke. She knew he wouldn't approve of what she'd done. That was *exactly* why she hadn't told him about her plan.

> What are you doing all the way out there? I'll call you.

Her breath caught.

> No! Don't call. Bad time.

A couple of seconds of silence passed. Andi could only imagine Duke's mind whirling as he tried to put the pieces together.

Finally, he typed:

> You can tell me more later. I'm on my way.

She let out a breath, thankful she could always count on Duke. She nibbled on her lip before typing the last part.

> I'm in a black van. Be subtle when you catch up. Stay back, and don't announce your arrival. Text when you're close.

A couple more minutes of silence passed before he responded.

What kind of trouble have you gotten yourself into?

Andi nibbled on her lip again. Duke knew her a little too well.

I'll explain everything. But not now. Signing off.

She double-checked her location—which appeared to be about fifteen minutes outside Fairbanks—and then slid her phone back into her pocket.

Duke hadn't said where he was at the moment, but he lived in Fairbanks, and he shouldn't be too far away.

She hoped.

The men began singing an off-key version of "Friends in Low Places." At least they sounded happy. But she knew these men were dangerous.

They were large and bulky with multiple tattoos, including a few on their faces. They talked in grunts and smelled like . . . well, like moldy cheese.

The scent made her stomach churn.

She stared at the tub beside her.

With the noise of the singing in the front seat concealing any sounds she might make, she carefully lifted the lid.

Small metal discs stared back at her. Discs? They almost looked like batteries, only a little larger—probably the size of a penny.

She lifted the lid to another nearby tub.

Her throat tightened.

Guns. Lots of guns.

Another tub held some random photos.

Before she could investigate anymore, they pulled to a stop.

Andi's heart thumped harder.

"Let's unload," one of the men said. "Then we'll let the boss know we're here."

Unload? If they took out these tubs she was hiding behind, they'd see her.

Even though they might like to sing along with Garth Brooks songs and sound goofy, Andi knew these guys were bad news. She didn't want to think about what would happen if they got their hands on her.

She swallowed hard as she planned her next move.

She only hoped Duke was nearby when she executed it.

————

DUKE GRIPPED the steering wheel of his black Toyota 4Runner.

A bad feeling churned in his gut.

Andi was being vague, and the fact he couldn't call her only raised more questions.

Then there was the whole black van reference. What was that about?

He knew he didn't have time to waste. He needed to get to her.

He headed north of Fairbanks, surrounded by nothing but trees, gentle hills, and quickly fading sunlight. He passed a gas station/deli that sold amazing hand pies made by a local woman. A couple of derelict houses. An abandoned school bus that may have served as an RV at one time.

Where exactly was Andi? Why was she way out here?

He sighed. He couldn't wait to hear her explanation.

When his GPS showed he was only five hundred feet away from the pin indicating Andi's location, he slowed.

Just as he pulled in front of an old, abandoned four-story brick building, he spotted the black van Andi had mentioned.

Two thugs stood outside the vehicle—thugs with meaty arms, hard jaws, and guns at their waistbands.

His muscles tightened. Whatever was going on here, he didn't like it.

Andi was in the back of that van, wasn't she? Duke had no idea why she might be back there. But it was the only thing that made sense.

He stared at the scene another moment.

His jaw hardened when he saw the men open the doors at the back. If Andi was hiding inside, she was about to be discovered.

An idea materialized in his head.

He drew in a deep breath before putting his SUV back into Drive.

He headed toward the van and rolled down his window as he pulled up beside the men.

He plastered on an affable smile as he turned to the two thugs, who promptly scowled at him.

"Hey, guys," Duke started. "I'm hoping you can help me."

The men exchanged a glance before looking back at him.

"Whatdaya need?" the one with a missing front tooth asked.

Was that a whiff of . . . cheese Duke smelled coming from the man?

"My GPS just went berserk," Duke said, relieved to have their attention.

Behind them, he saw Andi appear at the open van doors. If he played his cards right, she could sneak out while he distracted the men. He just needed to keep their attention.

"I'm trying to find the Dalton Highway," Duke continued. "My friend broke down up that way, and now he doesn't have any cell service. I can't call him back."

The second man grunted. "I don't know why anyone would want to go there of their own free will."

"It was my friend's bucket list item," Duke explained with a shrug. "I don't get it either. Am I close?"

Andi quietly climbed out and began tiptoeing toward the building.

If she could get out of sight, maybe she could make a run for the woods and Duke could pick her up.

Missing Tooth began giving him directions, and Duke listened carefully, repeating things several times to keep their focus on him and buy Andi some time.

When she was out of sight, he grinned. "You've been a big help. Thank you so much."

The men grunted again before turning back toward the van.

Duke let out a breath.

Then he turned his SUV around in the gravel parking lot and headed back down the road—thankfully, Andi had gone that same direction.

He scanned the woods as he passed.

A quarter mile away, a woman popped out from between the trees waving her hands.

Andi.

He pulled up beside her. Wasting no time, she ran to the passenger door of his 4Runner and practically dove inside.

"Let's go." She tapped the dash.

Duke hit the accelerator and sped down the road before those guys realized what had just happened.

He stole a glance at Andi as the van disappeared in the distance. "You want to tell me what's going on?"

"Yes, but I need something to drink first." She fanned

her face. "The scent inside that van . . . I thought I was going to throw up."

"You mean the scent of pungent cheese mixed with dirty socks?"

She frowned. "That's the one. You can smell it on me?"

"A little. Your clothes and hair must have absorbed some of it."

"That's just . . . perfect." Her frown deepened, and she lifted the collar of her sweatshirt and took a sniff. Her face scrunched as if she might barf.

Duke let out a sigh and continued down the road. He'd have to wait to hear her explanation. He had a feeling it would be a good one.

For now, he pulled to a stop at the gas station he'd passed earlier.

At least maybe he could get a hand pie while he was here. People came from all over to buy the pies. Duke had eaten a cloudberry one once, and it had been delicious.

They walked inside the outdated place. The air smelled like a mix of fuel, fried chicken sitting under a warmer, and hot dogs roasting in a glass-enclosed griller. It certainly beat the overpowering scent of rancid gym socks that had rubbed off on Andi.

Duke wanted answers. But instead of pushing her, he decided to play on her terms. Besides, Andi wasn't one who could be persuaded to do anything she didn't want to do.

She grabbed a water from the refrigerated section, twisted the top off, threw her head back, and took a long drink.

When she was done, she used the sleeve of her black sweatshirt to wipe her mouth.

Duke wouldn't admit it, but he found her incredibly attractive in her all-black, cat-burglar-like attire. Dirt smudged her cheeks, and her blue eyes looked even more piercing with the dark clothing.

He forced himself to look away.

Only a few other people were in the gas station's restaurant right now. A TV in the corner blared the evening news, and a woman with gray hair piled up high on top of her head stood behind the counter watching them with a keen eye.

Andi let out a deep breath before turning to him. "I was following a lead about Victor, and I got myself into a bit of a pickle."

"A pickle?" Talk about understatement of the year. Irritation rushed through him. Part of him thought he should hold the emotion at bay. But the other part of him didn't care. "Did you see those guys? You weren't in a pickle. You were in a compacter about to be crushed."

When would Andi realize that he was there for her? That if she needed anything, he would drop whatever he was doing to help—before she got herself into trouble. Hadn't he proven that to her yet?

She offered a quick shrug. "It was just a hunch. I never

thought I'd be stuck in the back of the van or that those thugs would return so quickly before I could get out. Seriously, they only stepped away for five minutes, and then they were back. I think they work for Victor."

Duke raked a hand through his hair. "You could've been killed. You should have told me what you were planning to do."

Fire flashed in her eyes. "Like I said, I never anticipated this happening. Besides, Victor is my battle, not yours."

Duke stared at her another moment, thoughts ruminating inside him.

He cared about her. There was no need to deny it. Undeniable chemistry sparked between the two of them. Every time Duke was around her, he wanted to touch her. To be closer. To become a permanent part of her life.

But he also knew there were issues that needed to be resolved first. However, part of him feared those issues would never be resolved.

At what point did he decide to move on? Should he decide that his fiancée, who had been missing for two years, was never coming back? He asked himself that question every day.

And every day he still didn't have an answer.

He was so close to deciding to move on. In fact, just earlier today he'd been thinking that he and Andi needed to have another talk about things. That he was tired of not acting on the tension between them. That he was tired of his life being on hold.

Andi was an amazing woman. Smart. Brave. Gorgeous.

She'd been there for him time and time again, and her loyalty and friendship were unmatched.

He swallowed hard before finally saying, "Any battle of yours is a battle of mine also."

Andi set her water bottle on a shelf full of chips and turned to him, her hands on her hips as she stared up at him. "Like I've told you before, I don't want to pull you into my mess."

He stepped closer and stared down at her with equal intensity. "And, like I said before, any mess of yours is a mess of mine."

She glared back up at him. "Duke, you have enough things of your own to deal with."

"I'm quite capable of dealing with many problems at one time."

"I don't want you dealing with my problems."

Their gazes locked.

Electricity crackled between them.

Duke's gaze traveled from Andi's ice-blue eyes to her full lips.

Lips he'd wanted to kiss for a very long time.

Tension thrummed from them. The pull between them was so strong that he had a hard time resisting the urge to grab Andi and draw her toward him.

Especially when she licked her lips as she just did.

Maybe he should do it. Throw caution to the wind.

Forget about all the what-ifs he so often wrestled with. Maybe he should move on.

Andi didn't say anything. She only stared up at him with that same open look in her eyes.

Almost as if she was giving him permission.

Or daring him to make a move.

His heart pounded harder. "Andi . . ."

"Yes?" Her voice sounded soft and wispy—not her normal tone.

What did he want to say? He wasn't used to being uncertain. "I . . ."

Before he could finish his statement, a photo of a woman flashed on the TV screen behind Andi.

Duke nearly lost his breath as he jerked his gaze away from Andi.

No. It couldn't be.

The reporter on the screen talked about a woman wanted for the death of six people in California.

As he fully focused on the photo, the woman's features became clear.

He wasn't mistaken.

Everything began to spin around him.

The picture on the screen was that of Celeste Dawson . . . his fiancée, who'd been missing for two years.

three

ANDI RELEASED her breath as her body sagged with disappointment.

She'd been *sure* Duke was going to kiss her.

So much anticipation had built inside her that, when he pulled away, her chest physically ached with frustration.

They'd been flirting with the idea of being together for so long . . . but they had so many reasons why it was a bad idea. Lately, they'd been edging closer to the line. Touching each other every chance they got. Throwing playful jabs into each other's sides. Hands brushing a little too long. Shoulders against each other while watching TV.

For once, Andi had been willing to give in.

Duke too.

But then something had shifted.

What exactly had happened for Duke to change his mind so quickly?

She turned to see what he was staring at and blinked several times when she saw the pretty blonde on the screen.

The air left Andi's lungs.

That was . . . Celeste.

Was Andi seeing things?

No, she was certain Celeste was the woman in the photo. Duke had shown her a picture before. Plus, Andi had done her own research.

Then the words on the screen caught her eye.

Kelly Hanson.

Wanted for six counts of murder.

California.

Nationwide manhunt.

What?

But . . . Celeste had disappeared from Alaska two years ago. Before that, she'd been in Nebraska. She and Duke had met in Colorado.

So why . . . ?

She looked up at Duke. Saw how his face had gone pale. How his lips were parted. How his breathing seemed even more shallow.

Suddenly, Andi forgot about her questions. The reality of what Duke must be feeling slammed into her mind.

She squeezed his bicep. "Duke . . ."

He continued staring at the TV until the news story switched to something else.

But he still looked stunned and almost listless as he processed all the details, shock frozen on his expression.

"Duke," she repeated.

Finally, he snapped out of his daze. Ran a hand through his dark hair. Shuffled his feet. Ran his hand through his hair again.

"I . . . I don't know what to think," he finally muttered.

"Did Celeste ever live in California?"

He shook his head. "No. At least, she didn't tell me she did."

"So she lied to you." That was what the news story indicated.

He raised his chin defensively. "Or the police have the wrong person. That couldn't be Celeste. She would never kill anyone. I need to find out more information."

His loyalty ran deep.

Andi pushed down a surge of . . . what was that emotion? Jealousy? She wasn't sure.

Jealousy was the last thing she wanted to feel. It had no place in her life. It was an emotion for weak-minded people. That was what her dad had always said.

Instead, she tried to focus on the tangible. On finding answers.

"I can call Gibson," she offered. "He needs to know about this. If he doesn't already."

Duke didn't argue.

Andi pulled out her phone, ready to call the state trooper. As she searched for his number, she grabbed her water and sauntered toward the counter. Before she walked away, she saw Duke type something into his own phone.

No doubt he was looking up more details about this new investigation.

Gibson answered on the second ring.

"It's Andi," she started, pausing at the counter, and setting her water there.

"Funny, you called," Gibson said. "I was just about to dial Duke."

Andi slid a five-dollar bill to the cashier and mouthed for her to keep the change. The woman grabbed the money, waved it in the air, and nodded in affirmation.

"You heard the news?" Andi turned to head back to Duke.

"I did. About an hour before it hit the news stations. I just got off the phone with the FBI. I had no choice but to let them know about my investigation two years ago. An agent is heading to Fairbanks now. Where are you now?"

"I'm at a gas station with Duke. We're about fifteen minutes away from his place."

"We need him to meet us there," Gibson said.

Andi glanced at Duke, worried about the toll that all this would take on him. "Understandable."

He was about to go through some grueling hours of questioning. Rehashing the events leading up to Celeste's disappearance. Their relationship. That was just the tip of the iceberg. He'd have to relive his loss. His confusion. New details could also be revealed, details that could devastate him.

None of this would be easy.

Andi only knew that, above all else, she needed to be there for Duke.

Just like he'd been there for her throughout all this craziness as she searched for answers about Victor.

She ended the call with Gibson and took Duke's arm. "Come on. We need to go."

———

DUKE CLIMBED into the passenger seat.

Andi had insisted that she drive, and he didn't argue. It wouldn't be safe for him to be behind the wheel, not with his thoughts racing like they were.

Andi adjusted the seat, pulling it a good six or seven inches closer to the wheel. Then she repositioned the rearview mirror and turned the heat on. Even though it was the end of summer, it felt chilly tonight with temperatures in the fifties.

A moment later, she started down the road.

He preferred to drive, but he'd ridden with Andi enough to know she was a safe driver.

Even if she wasn't, Duke wasn't sure he cared right now.

He felt like someone else had taken over his body, like his thoughts had become a separate person of their own.

All he could think about was Celeste. Her image on that screen. The accusations against her.

"What did you find out?" Andi turned the radio down and "Bad Romance" faded as she gave him her full attention.

"Apparently, these murders happened more than four years ago." Which meant this happened before Duke had even met Celeste.

"Four years ago?" Andi stole a glance at him. "And she's just now been named as a suspect?"

He shrugged. "I'm not sure why. But I think one of the articles said some new evidence had come to light."

She pursed her lips. "You two dated a year, right? And she's been missing two years."

Duke nodded, still trying to put together both the pieces and the timeline himself.

"So that means these murders happened right before you all got together . . ."

"Apparently." He was still trying to make sense of that. Celeste had supposedly lived in Nebraska when they met, where she'd worked as a traveling nurse. She'd said she grew up in Arizona. California had never been mentioned. "One of the news articles called her Nursy Mercy."

"Why?" Andi asked.

His throat tightened, but he continued the conversation. "Six people, each with life-altering diagnoses, who were hospitalized in Burbank, California, died while under Celeste's care. At first, their deaths were believed to be from natural causes. But authorities have been investigating—for a while now, apparently. They discovered that these patients were actually given a lethal dose of a medication called curare. Since they were already sick, their deaths weren't investigated—until now."

"So they were mercy killings."

"That's what the news said." Duke swung his head back and forth vehemently. "Celeste wouldn't do something like that."

"There has to be more to it."

Of all the scenarios Duke had put together in his mind of what might have happened to Celeste, never was this one of them.

"None of this makes sense." The more he tried to make sense of things, the more his temples pounded.

Maybe Gibson would have some answers for him.

Duke trusted the man. He was a good cop. He'd been on the case when Celeste disappeared, so he knew the ins and outs of the investigation.

Duke hoped the state trooper might shed some light on things.

Andi pulled to a stop in a parking space in front of Duke's condo.

Gibson's SUV was already outside, another dark sedan parked beside it.

The FBI?

Maybe.

If they thought Celeste was a killer who'd crossed state lines, the feds would definitely want to get involved.

He dreaded the conversation about to take place. Dreaded what he might learn. Dreaded a reality he might not want to face.

What if his fiancée really was a killer?

four

AS SOON AS Duke and Andi stepped out of the SUV, Gibson and a tall man with pale skin and ginger hair appeared.

"Special Agent O'Brian with the FBI," the other man said with a nod. "I'm here from DC to take lead in this investigation."

"Duke McAllister." Duke nodded beside him. "And this is Andi Slade."

"Thanks for meeting with us," Agent O'Brian said.

"Of course." Duke gestured toward his bright red front door. "Come on inside."

Duke unlocked the door to his condo and ushered them into his home. He didn't bother to offer water or coffee. Formalities seemed meaningless right now.

They all took seats in the living room. Duke appreciated that Andi sat beside him on his leather couch, silently offering her support.

Silent *for now*. He knew Andi well enough to know she'd speak up if inclined.

Before Gibson or O'Brian could start, Duke turned toward them. "What can you tell me?"

O'Brian nodded at Gibson, giving him the go-ahead. Gibson shifted, the sleeve of his uniform slipping up to reveal a tattoo. The man had always seemed more like a rebel than a cop—maybe that's why they got along so well.

He'd been stationed up in the North Slope borough when Celeste went missing and had only recently been reassigned to the Fairbanks area.

"I'm going to be honest. I don't know much more than what was already on the news."

O'Brian shifted. "As you may or may not have seen, this woman's real name is Kelly Hanson. We've been searching for her, but it appears she changed her name when she moved from California to Nebraska and then to Alaska. Because of that, we were unable to trace her until Gibson recognized her photo on our newly released most wanted list and contacted us."

"Why do you think she's guilty?" Duke had so many questions, and he wasn't sure why that was the first one that popped into his head. But it was.

"A great amount of evidence has recently come to light," Agent O'Brian said, his expression stoic.

"Could you share what?" Andi sat still and poised beside him, listening with rapt attention.

The agent hesitated before saying, "We investigated the death of one of the victims after a family member begged local authorities to investigate. The body was finally exhumed, and an autopsy was done."

"And?"

"This family member was right. The death wasn't natural at all. There were traces of curare in his system, which indicates he was indeed murdered. Unfortunately, the family member who set this all in motion died in a car accident a month before the exhumation."

"And you think Kelly/Celeste is responsible?" Duke's voice wavered as he asked the question.

O'Brian nodded. "Hanson was the last person to treat him before his untimely death. We then began looking into other patients who died under her care, and that's when we discovered her string of murders that, at first glance, appeared to be from natural causes."

"Did you exhume all the bodies?" Andi asked.

The agent nodded again. "The ones we could. There could be more victims, but others were cremated."

"She didn't do it." Duke's words were edged with certainty.

O'Brian's gaze locked with Duke's. "Do you have any idea where she is?"

Duke shook his head. "I've been looking for her for two years. Gibson probably told you that."

"He mentioned it." O'Brian shifted. "Said you thought you saw her a few months ago."

Duke shrugged. "Her or someone who looked like her. I haven't been able to figure out which yet."

"She's your fiancée, and you're not sure it was her?" O'Brian raised an eyebrow.

Duke bristled. "It's not that simple."

"Did she ever mention she'd lived in California?" Gibson asked, his voice friendlier and less accusatory than O'Brian's.

"No, she didn't."

"Did she even hint at it?" O'Brian's razor-sharp gaze remained on Duke.

At once, a memory hit Duke, but he held it back. He needed to think things through more before he shared anything that may or may not be helpful.

He swallowed hard. "No, no hints of it even. I'd say you could talk to her family but, as you probably already know, her parents are dead and she's an only child. At least, that's what she told me. Who knows what the truth is? She never mentioned any cousins or other relatives."

"Do you have any of her personal belongings?" O'Brian waited for his answer.

"I do," Duke said. "They're in a storage unit here in town."

"We're going to need to see those belongings," O'Brian said.

"Of course. Whatever you need to find her." Duke's throat tightened. "But Celeste isn't a killer."

"These were mercy killings." O'Brian lowered his voice. "The person behind them probably thought she was doing the right thing."

Duke shook his head. "Even so, Celeste wouldn't kill anyone. She doesn't have it in her."

"It seems like there's a lot you didn't know about your fiancée," O'Brian said. "Starting with her real name."

Duke's throat tightened. He couldn't argue, not given this new information. But he didn't appreciate the man's tone. "So you're telling me that Celeste murdered these people in California and then changed her name and fled, all in order not to be caught?"

O'Brian nodded, not appearing in the least to think the story was outlandish. "That's the working theory."

"But no one even suspected her?"

"She could have run because of a guilty conscience or even as a preemptive measure," Gibson suggested.

"Then maybe someone came poking around and spooked her while she was in Fairbanks, and that's why she went missing and is on the run again. Because she feared being discovered."

Duke's thoughts raced. "But if the police found her in Alaska, it seems they would have questioned me somewhere in the process."

"Maybe it wasn't the police." O'Brian raised a faint

eyebrow. "Maybe it was a family member of one of her victims. It's hard to say until we know more details."

Duke let out a long breath.

A family member of one of the victims? It was something to consider.

There was so much he needed to consider.

And so much he prayed wasn't true.

———

ANDI HAD TRIED to listen without drawing conclusions as Gibson and O'Brian spoke with them. There was clearly more going on here than met the eye.

Right now, Gibson and O'Brian were going to meet them at the storage unit. Duke had already given them the address, and the two men had stepped outside.

But before Duke followed them out, Andi grabbed his arm.

Grief emanated from him, and she could only imagine how difficult this was for him.

There were things she wanted to say to him, things she didn't want others to hear.

But also things she felt couldn't wait.

"Hey . . . I'm sorry this is happening, Duke." The words sounded lame given the scope of the situation. But what else should she say?

Duke's troubled gaze met hers, and he offered a stiff nod.

She wanted more than anything to pull him into a hug. To offer some type of comfort.

But right now, he didn't seem receptive.

Before she could ponder something deeper or more life-changing to say, he opened the door and stepped outside, clearly anxious to get to that storage unit.

She could understand his need for answers.

"I'm okay to drive this time," Duke called over his shoulder. "Some of the shock has worn off, and we're only going up the road."

Andi held back a frown. "If you're sure . . ."

He unlocked the door to his 4Runner, readjusted the seat, and then climbed in. Andi scrambled into the passenger seat. Just as she clicked on her seatbelt, her phone buzzed.

She glanced at the screen and saw a message from Mariella Boucher. Mariella headed up The Round Table, the true crime podcast Andi and Duke were part of. She was trying to get the team together for a meeting. This weekend was the one the team normally set aside for their monthly gathering.

Had Mariella seen the news story on Celeste? Did she know what was going on with Duke?

Are you still good for tomorrow?

Andi stared at the message. She didn't even know how to respond.

Andi knew Duke didn't want to go to the meeting. He was already on the outs with Mariella after some philosophical differences on how things were done in the murder club. But now with this new Celeste development . . .

Andi slipped the phone back into her pocket. She would wait to answer. This wasn't the time to even bring up the meeting with Duke, not when there were so many other things they needed to concentrate on.

Just as Duke had said, the storage facility was only a few minutes down the street. He punched his code in at the gate, and it opened. He drove through first, Gibson and O'Brian following behind him.

They pulled to a stop in front of Unit 115.

Andi didn't know why, but nausea swirled in her gut as Duke unlocked the door to the storage space.

The fact that he'd saved all of Celeste's things was just another reminder to her that he'd been deeply in love with the woman. That maybe he still was. That maybe in the process of defending Celeste against these allegations, Duke would be reminded of just how strong those feelings were.

Maybe this would be the opportunity he needed in order to find her again.

Those earlier thoughts Andi had toyed with about her and Duke finally being able to be together disappeared from her mind like the aurora on a cloudy night.

The roll-up door slid open, and Duke reached for the wall to flip on the light.

Boxes appeared inside.

But they'd all been torn open. The contents were strewn all over the space.

Duke wouldn't leave Celeste's things like this. He kept things orderly.

Someone had been in here recently.

Someone who'd been looking for something.

Andi swallowed hard.

Most likely, they'd been looking for ways to find Celeste.

five

DUKE FELT as if he were watching himself out-of-body as he went through the boxes—with O'Brian's permission, of course.

He definitely hadn't left this place like this. He liked organization and had kept the boxes neatly stacked on top of each other with everything inside.

Someone had done this—and recently, at that.

"When was the last time you were here?" O'Brian glanced around as he asked the question.

He hesitated before saying, "A couple of weeks ago."

He didn't look at Andi. Didn't know what she'd think about that statement.

Of course, she knew he was still looking for Celeste. But what Andi didn't know was that Duke liked to come here sometimes to try to sort things out. To look for hints as to what might have happened to Celeste.

It wasn't necessarily because he still had feelings for Celeste. The situation was complicated, to say the least.

But he could understand why Andi might hear that and think his feelings for her were all a lie.

They weren't.

"Have you noticed anything missing?" Gibson stood close, watching Duke work.

"Not yet. I didn't make a detailed list of what was here, though. I know Celeste's clothes were in those six boxes. Her toiletries and makeup were in another. I put all her books in another box and all her files in this one." He tapped the top of the box in front of him as he sat on the floor.

Her files seemed the most likely things that might have been gone through.

Duke had looked through them himself so many times. One would think he'd have memorized everything in this unit. But he hadn't. Hadn't thought he should. Hadn't thought his investigation would ever lead to this.

As he began to rifle through the files, O'Brian dug through several other boxes. Gibson stood guard at the door. And Andi sat beside Duke in more of a supportive role.

He paused at a file full of notes he'd handwritten to Celeste. A smile tried to creep across his face, but he stopped it. There was no need to indulge in sweet memories. Not now. Not with so many uncertainties.

But the two of them had experienced some great times

together. They'd been deeply in love and ready to spend the rest of their lives with one another. They'd had plans to honeymoon in Hawaii. To travel to Greece for their one-year anniversary. To save up to buy a house with a couple acres of land, where Celeste could plant all the lilies she wanted—it was her favorite flower. They'd wanted to have two children.

As he started to close the folder, a picture slipped out. A selfie Duke took of himself planting a kiss on Celeste's cheek. Her face was radiant, her eyes glowing, and her smile wide.

She looked nothing like a killer.

Duke felt Andi's gaze on him and slid the photo back into the folder and closed it.

Time to move on.

He paused at a file labeled *Warranty Information*.

On top was some paperwork for her car and more paperwork for a wedding ring.

A wedding ring?

Duke kept reading.

Celeste had picked out his ring, he realized. Was she going to surprise him? Because he'd had no idea. He'd assumed they'd go shopping together.

An ache filled his chest.

He didn't know what to make of that, so he cast the thought aside.

He flipped open the next folder and paused.

He squinted, unsure if he was seeing this correctly.

Then he realized he was.

They were medical files.

From patients at Northwest Regional Hospital in Burbank, California.

His pulse sped.

No. This couldn't be what he was seeing.

Because if it was . . . it was confirmation of Celeste's past life.

He refused to believe she'd been that woman. Nursy Mercy.

O'Brian seemed to sense his surprise and stepped closer. "What's that?"

Duke swallowed hard before looking up. "These appear to be medical records."

"For whom?"

Duke read the names on each of the six sheets. People he'd never heard of. People who'd been patients in Burbank.

"The victims," Gibson announced, his jaw hardening. "Those are the names of the victims."

A hollow feeling formed in Duke's stomach. "These weren't here before."

O'Brian eyed him. "Are you sure?"

"I'm positive."

"Did you have this storage unit before Celeste disappeared?" Gibson asked.

"I did."

"Did she know how to get inside?" Gibson continued.

"She did." Duke knew how this sounded. Even he couldn't deny how guilty Celeste looked.

"Maybe these documents were here all along, but you thought they were unimportant and skipped over them," Andi suggested.

"I went through every bit of this paperwork. Someone has been here. These records, as well as the file with the ring information . . . they were absolutely *not* in this storage facility earlier." His gaze locked with O'Brian's as one thought settled in his head. "Somebody is trying to set Celeste up."

———

ANDI HEARD the protectiveness in Duke's voice.

She'd been sure he was over Celeste.

She'd been wrong.

A weight pressed on her heart at the thought. Andi had reminded herself not to get close. She'd told herself she should play it safe.

But clearly, her heart had other ideas.

Duke had eased his way into her life as effortlessly as snow melting under the late spring sunshine.

Duke finally stood and helped Andi to her feet. She wished she didn't feel a tangible electricity at his touch, but she did.

She ignored it. Electricity and fireworks were for losers.

Not really. But she prided herself on her reasoning skills. She needed to tap into them now instead of dwelling on her feelings.

For a long time, Andi had known that Duke could stand up next to any of the cowboys she'd dated back in Texas. None of them had ever held her interest for long. None of them had made her want to consider a relationship.

No one until Duke.

Now she was hoping for the impossible. The realization seemed fitting for her risk-taking personality.

Just then, another vehicle pulled to a stop outside, and four FBI agents climbed out. They flooded the storage area.

Duke turned back to O'Brian, his face all grim lines and grief. "Any more questions?"

"Not now. But if you think of anything . . ." The FBI agent handed him a card.

"I'll call," Duke finished.

He moved out of the way as agents began to dig through the remnants of his relationship with Celeste. Andi's heart thudded into her chest as she watched. This had to make Duke feel as if scabs were being ripped off old wounds.

Gibson gave them a nod, compassion in his gaze as he watched Andi and Duke slip past.

Even though Andi thought of Gibson as a friend, he

still had a job to do. It was better if he kept his distance and remained professional in this situation.

They climbed into the SUV, Duke in the driver's seat again.

As soon as they pulled away from the storage unit, Andi said, "You remembered something about Celeste in California earlier, didn't you? When you were in the condo."

He stole a glance at her. "How did you know?"

"I can read you."

He hesitated another minute before saying, "Once, Celeste started telling this story. It was about a patient she had who kept walking around the hospital naked. She told him if he kept doing that, Hollywood was the only one who'd want to hire him—but not the side of Hollywood he was looking for. I asked her, 'why Hollywood?' It seemed like a leap, you know?"

"And?"

"Celeste looked flustered for a few seconds before shrugging and telling me the man wanted to be an actor. Then she said, 'I told him Nebraska isn't the best place for someone trying to break into showbiz.'" Duke frowned. "Looking back at that conversation, I wonder if it was an accidental slip she tried to correct."

"But if she's innocent, why hide the fact she lived there?"

"That's what I'm trying to figure out." He pulled to a

stop in front of his condo, but neither of them made a move to get out.

Andi licked her lips before asking, "What now?"

"I need to find Celeste before the FBI does and figure out what's going on. It's more urgent now than ever."

"I hate to be the one to remind you of this, but you've been searching for her for two years with no luck."

"She did show up at your apartment once," Duke reminded her. "And we may have found where she was living."

"Maybe," she reminded him. "We don't have any proof that woman was Celeste—only that she looked like her. What makes you think something will be different now? If she's hiding, she'll only go deeper."

His jaw hardened. "I know. But these potential new developments add more layers to everything. I need to keep trying."

She heard the determination in his voice and didn't argue. "You want me to stay here tonight? Sleep on the couch in case you need something?"

She could see where he might not want to be alone. That he might need someone to turn to for a shoulder to cry on or a listening ear.

Duke offered a tight smile. "Thanks for the offer, but I'll be fine."

Andi rubbed her throat, feeling something shifting between them. A wall had gone up, and she knew that wall needed to be there—at least until some things were figured out.

"If that's what you want," she told him. "But could you drop me off at my car? It's downtown."

He raised his eyebrows. "Downtown?"

"Near an old warehouse-type place." She shrugged as if it weren't a big deal.

The whole incident with the black van now felt like something that had happened weeks ago.

Funny how trauma could do that—and trauma was *exactly* what this was. Maybe not so much for her but for Duke.

She gave him directions, and several minutes later, he pulled to a stop beside her car.

Her mind flashed back to that man who'd been beaten.

He wasn't here any longer. And the fact that the police weren't here scouring the scene meant he'd probably gotten away.

Andi would have to follow up sometime. Try to figure out why this man was working for Victor.

But not right now.

Duke turned toward her. "I still have a lot of questions about you and how you ended up in that black van."

"I know. And I'll explain it all. But right now, you have other things to think about."

His gaze locked with hers. "Don't do anything stupid tonight. Promise me."

An almost pleading sound filled his voice, as if he couldn't handle anything else.

Andi nodded reassuringly. "I won't."

"And just a heads-up—I'm going to follow you home, just to make sure nothing else happens."

Warmth filled Andi's chest. It felt good to have someone watching her back, even if she didn't want to admit it. "Only if you insist."

As she started to climb into the car, she paused and glanced around.

Goosebumps popped up across her arms.

Why did she feel as if someone were watching her?

She scanned everything around her but didn't see anything that raised any red flags.

Quickly, she ducked into her car.

As soon as she slammed the door, her cell phone rang. An unknown number with a local area code came across the screen.

Sometimes—most of the time—she didn't answer unrecognizable numbers. For some reason, this time she did.

She put the phone to her ear. "Hello?"

Silence stretched on the other end, except for the sound of light breathing and static.

Someone was there. They just weren't speaking.

Was this a bad connection? Or was there something more to it?

"Hello?" Andi repeated, glancing around to make sure no one was watching.

That eerie feeling crept up her spine again.

Still, she saw no one.

But the same light breathing and static filled the line.

"I . . . need . . . you . . . Duke," a scattered voice said. "Please."

A woman's voice.

Another thought hit Andi.

This was Celeste, wasn't it?

six

Then

PATIENT 502 OPENED HER EYES.

Tried to move.

But she couldn't.

She tried again to force her eyelids apart. This time she was successful.

A bright light shone above her. She squinted against the glare.

Had she been abducted by aliens?

No, that thought was absurd. She didn't even believe in extraterrestrial beings.

So what was going on?

Then memories slammed into her mind.

She knew *exactly* what was happening.

Terror squeezed her lungs.

She turned her head away from the overhead light as her thoughts raced.

That was when she saw someone wearing a surgical gown, mask, and goggles.

Despite the gear, she knew it was a woman.

She knew exactly who the woman was.

Nurse Reaper. Though it wasn't her real name, that was what everyone at the clinic called her.

What would happen next became exceedingly clear to her.

She had to stop it . . .

Now. Before it was too late.

She tugged at her arms, desperate to get away.

But her wrists were bound to the gurney with cuffs.

Panic surged through her.

"Hi there," Nurse Reaper crooned.

She'd thought the nurse was so nice when they'd first met. But the woman had everyone fooled.

"I was hoping you might stay asleep so we could get started," Reaper said.

"Please, don't do this."

"Oh, sweetie . . ." Reaper rubbed her hair back. "I know this is difficult. But it won't be that bad. I promise."

"I've seen what happens. Please, if you have any ounce of goodness in you, don't do this."

"I'm all about goodness." Reaper smiled with her eyes. "In fact, I consider this very merciful."

"But you're doing it against my will." Her mind raced. She'd suspected this was going on. Then she'd discovered the truth. Now she would become another victim.

"This will all be over with soon," Reaper murmured.

She fought against her restraints again. As she did, she saw others in the shadows. Those who would help Nurse Reaper do her thing.

Reaper moved toward her IV. Checked a few stats on it. Then she pulled out a needle.

Cold fear spread through her.

No amount of talking would get her out of this situation. She knew that.

She was hopeless.

And at the nurse's mercy.

"Please . . ." she murmured one last time.

"I'm sorry," Reaper muttered. "But there's a purpose for this. One day, after you're dead, people will thank you."

"You won't get away with this." She watched with wide eyes as the needle was inserted into the IV's cannula.

Sweat spread across her forehead. Ice filled her veins. Her lungs tightened until she couldn't breathe.

"Just give it a few minutes, and this will be all over with."

"No . . ." she murmured again as desperation raced through her.

Then everything blurred around her.

She tried to fight it. Tried to think of arguments that would get her out of this.

But there was nothing.

Nothing.

Nothing . . .

Then everything went black.

seven
Now

DUKE HAD HARDLY SLEPT.

Instead, he'd paced his condo. Researched on his computer. Prayed long and hard.

Gibson had called. Said they checked security footage at the storage facility. A week ago, someone had gone into his unit. Unfortunately, the cameras weren't great, and cops couldn't identify the person—not even if it was a man or a woman.

Duke thought several times about calling Andi. But he hadn't. It didn't seem fair to Andi for Duke to pull her into this mess, especially since he didn't know what the outcome would be.

Of course, that was Andi's reasoning for not telling him about whatever she'd been up to tonight, a scenario where she might have been seriously hurt or even killed.

He shoved that thought aside for now.

Would he ever find Celeste? Did she need him?

At what point did he let this go and move on? Should he cut his losses? Realize that Celeste may have never really cared about him?

Despite all his pacing and thinking and praying, he still had no answers. He managed to lie down a couple of hours and try to rest, but it was useless. All his dreams were about Celeste.

They'd been nightmares, really.

Had his fiancée been a killer?

He just couldn't reconcile the thought of Celeste, a nurse, also being a murderer.

Yet everything that happened over the past couple of years proved she had some type of secret she was hiding.

She must have had a good reason.

Which then left him at his earlier theory.

Someone had set her up.

He shoved those thoughts aside as he tried to get ready for the day.

He'd barely started to brush his teeth when a knock sounded at the door. He rinsed his mouth before lumbering through the condo and peering through the peephole.

Andi stood on the other side.

His heart lifted—though it shouldn't.

He opened the door and ushered her inside, taking notes of the cardboard container with two coffee cups and a paper bag in her hands.

"I brought coffee and donuts." She raised them higher. "Thought you might need a little pick-me-up."

"You're the best," he muttered.

Then Duke wondered if he should have said that.

He was normally sure of himself. Doubting every word and thought threw him off-kilter.

They sat at his small kitchen table, and he took the coffee from his favorite shop in Fairbanks. It was black, just like he liked it.

Andi opened the bag and pulled out four donuts, setting them on the wax paper they'd been dispensed in. "I got all different kinds, not knowing which one you might be in the mood for today. Chunky Monkey? Lucky Charms? Banana Split? Or just a plain chocolate?"

"I'm feeling like this is a Chunky Monkey kind of day." He picked up the doughnut. The truth was he didn't have much of an appetite. But he would eat something—though he wasn't sure a doughnut was the best idea.

As he took a bite, Andi studied him from across the table, not touching the doughnuts herself. But her fingers clutched the paper coffee cup in her hands. "Did you get any sleep?"

"Do I look that bad?"

She shrugged. "You look a little rough."

"It wasn't the best of nights."

"I can only imagine." She pressed her lips together.

Duke could tell she had something she wanted to say, but she hesitated.

He paused, his gaze meeting hers. "What is it?"

She swallowed hard and rubbed her throat. "This might be nothing. But I don't want to keep secrets from you."

He set his doughnut down, suddenly not interested at all in eating. "What is it?"

"I got a phone call last night. It was a bad connection, but I made out the words 'I, need, you, Duke, and please.' It was a woman's voice, and I couldn't help but think that it might be . . ."

"Celeste?"

Compassion flooded Andi's pale blue eyes as she nodded. "I know it sounds crazy."

Duke's thoughts whirred. "Celeste did reach out to you at your apartment that time. At least, it was a woman we *think* was Celeste."

Someone who looked like Celeste had come to Andi's apartment when she wasn't home. The woman had been wearing a baseball cap that shadowed her features.

Duke had tried to talk to her through the doorbell camera. He'd asked the woman if she was Celeste.

The visitor had looked up, startled as if she recognized his voice.

In the video, Duke couldn't tell if the woman was bruised or disheveled after being treated poorly. He couldn't tell if she was under duress or there by her own free will.

A handwritten note had been left that said, *Stay out of this.*

Was Celeste trying to protect Andi? Or herself? Had she been warning her away?

Or what if the woman hadn't been Celeste at all, just a lookalike? Someone trying to play mind tricks on him?

But why would someone do that?

The whole incident was still a mystery.

Duke's gaze focused on Andi again. "Why would Celeste call you?"

"I'm not sure." Her thumbs rubbed the side of her coffee cup. "Calling you would probably be too risky. She has to know the police are talking to you."

"Maybe." Duke leaned back in his seat, his thoughts still racing.

Andi fidgeted again, something clearly on her mind. Duke didn't push her to share. She would when she was ready.

Finally, she said, "Listen, Duke . . . Mariella would really like for us all to get together today at the hotel."

Without a second of consideration, he shook his head. "I don't want to go."

"She just saw the story on the news about Celeste," Andi continued. "She wants to help."

"She *always* wants to help. But there are strings attached. Those strings are starting to strangle me."

"I know you're frustrated with her, and I understand you two have some philosophical differences on this. I really do."

"*Mariella and I* have differences?" He stared at Andi. "Are you saying that you're on board with everything she suggests?"

"No, I think we need to set more ground rules to ensure we're all on the same page."

"Have we ever all been on the same page?" His voice rose. "Just think of that contract she convinced us all to sign with Alpine Grist."

The edges of Andi's mouth pulled down in a frown. "Well, that's part of the reason she wants to meet. We're contractually obligated to do one podcast together a month. Doesn't mean you have to like it. But it does mean you have to participate."

He narrowed his eyes, fighting irritation. "I need to look for Celeste."

"Mariella knows that. She wants us all to get involved. You've got to admit it could be a good idea in light of this new evidence. We can get Matthew to trace that phone call to me last night. We can have Ranger and Simmy look into Nursy Mercy's victims. I think it's a good idea. The last thing you need right now is to be alone. You need your team around you."

His team? Convincing wording.

Andi's past as a lawyer came in handy sometimes.

His gaze met hers. "If I agree to do this, I definitely want to set these ground rules you mentioned."

"Of course." Andi nodded, her gaze earnest.

Duke let out a long sigh before rising. "Okay. Let me get changed, and then we'll go. You can let Mariella know."

———

AS DUKE WAS in the shower, Andi straightened up his condo, throwing away their trash from breakfast and fluffing his pillow on the couch. It made her feel like she was doing *something*.

As she reached for another navy-blue pillow, a noise sounded outside his condo.

Her back muscles tightened.

She set the pillow back down and paced to the window, carefully nudging the curtain aside.

A lump formed in her throat at what she saw.

Two news vans had parked outside Duke's place.

Reporters must have caught wind that Nursy Mercy had used a different name and come to Alaska, where she'd been engaged to Duke.

Now they wanted information from him.

Duke wouldn't handle this well.

The pressure would only cause added stress in an already stressful situation. Andi knew how reporters could be. Aggressive. Hungry. Relentless.

They would badger Duke until they got what they wanted.

Except Duke wasn't the type to give in out of pressure. But still.

He stepped out of his bedroom a few seconds later dressed in some jeans and a long-sleeved black T-shirt. His hair was still damp, and he hadn't bothered to shave.

Andi liked the unshaven look on him. The shadow across his jaw. The rugged way it made clean-cut Duke look.

Not that it mattered right now. In fact, it mattered less now than it ever did. With Celeste back in the picture, Andi needed to quickly kill any attraction she felt to Duke.

"What's going on?" He paused and gave her a curious glance.

"We're going to want to go out the back way." She nodded toward the small patio off his dining room.

"Who's out there?" He started toward the front door, but Andi grabbed his arm.

"Reporters. Two vans, but there will probably be more coming."

Heat rose in his gaze. "How do they even know who I am?"

"You know how gossip can spread."

He ran a hand from his jaw to the back of his neck, which he then started to knead. "Unfortunately, I do."

"We won't be able to use your 4Runner," Andi told

him. "I've already called Ranger and Simmy. They're going to pick us up in a different lot."

Duke cast a quick but faint smile her way. "What would I do without you?"

Andi ignored the surge of warmth she felt at his question. His tone was filled with so much affection that she wanted to bask in it.

But she couldn't.

Instead, she cleared her throat. "We should probably get moving. Ranger and Simmy will be here in about five minutes."

They walked to his back patio and opened the door. When they did, Andi paused. An envelope waited on the patio, Duke's name scrawled across the front.

Andi had seen that handwriting before.

Most recently, last night in the storage unit.

It looked a lot like Celeste's.

eight

DUKE CAREFULLY PICKED up the envelope and stared at it.

That was Celeste's handwriting. He would recognize it anywhere.

He glanced around, looking for any signs she'd been here—or that she was still close.

Everything looked normal.

A ruckus sounded from the front yard.

Reporters, he realized. They were now pounding at his door, impatient about getting their quote or headline.

Andi placed her hand on his forearm, sending a jolt through him.

"We need to go," she murmured. "We can't stay here any longer. You can open that later."

He pressed his lips together before nodding. She was right.

He tucked the envelope into the back pocket of his jeans and started toward the privacy fence.

Andi cracked the gate open and glanced around. Then she motioned for him to follow.

They cut across a couple of streets until they reached one at the back of the condo complex. They lingered out of sight near the community mailboxes waiting for Ranger and Simmy to arrive.

Not wanting to waste a moment, Duke ripped open the envelope.

A simple white card rested inside with a handwritten message across it.

Meet me tonight at 9:30 at our special place.
Come alone.

Duke's heart began to beat double-time.

Celeste wanted to meet? Was this real?

"Duke . . ." Andi's voice cut into his thoughts.

He glanced up but said nothing. He knew what she was thinking, and part of him didn't want to hear what she had to say. Didn't want his hopes to be doused.

Instead, she asked, "What's your special place? Is that real?"

Memories pummeled him. "Celeste and I used to go to this spot at the university where, on clear days, you can see Denali."

Andi nodded slowly, any emotion she might be feeling

masked in her gaze. "Why would Celeste risk everything to come to your condo and leave that note? Her face is all over the news. The FBI is here. Reporters. It's too risky."

His temples began to throb. Andi had a point. Maybe someone else had delivered that note for Celeste. But even so, no one else knew about their secret spot.

Only he and Celeste.

Unless . . . maybe Celeste had mentioned the Denali overlook to someone somewhere along the way. But that was all a guessing game. He couldn't let himself drown in the what-ifs.

But he did need to address those scenarios. It was only wise.

"But what if it *was* her?" he asked.

Andi's calm gaze met his. "Your emotions are running high right now. If someone's setting Celeste up . . . someone could be setting you up also. You need to think this through. *Really* think this through."

He *would* think this through.

But he already knew he'd see what this was all about. Celeste—or someone else—was toying with him.

Duke needed to find out the truth.

AS RANGER GARRETT and Simmy Samuels pulled up in Ranger's Tahoe, Andi felt relief sweep through her.

They were a good distraction.

Because Andi knew by looking at Duke's face that he was considering the idea Celeste really had left this note and she really wanted to meet him.

But Andi had meant what she'd told him. There was no good reason for Celeste to take a risk like this, especially not when there were other ways to communicate like via text, phone call, or social media.

Celeste coming to his condo to leave that note was absolutely out of the question.

But Duke was too immersed in his grief right now to see that. Or maybe grief wasn't the right word. Maybe it was hope.

Hope was a tough pill for Andi to swallow. At the same time, it was a necessary one. Andi couldn't stick her head in the sand and pretend Duke didn't have feelings for Celeste. She couldn't be offended by those feelings or pretend they weren't real.

The whole situation was entirely complicated, and she'd known that from the start. She just needed to keep reminding herself of that fact.

She and Duke climbed into the back of the Tahoe and said their greetings to Ranger and Simmy.

The two had recently begun dating, and Andi couldn't be happier for her friends. Former CIA operative Ranger and nurturing, sweet Simmy. They seemed to truly be a good match.

"Thanks for the ride," Andi said as she snapped her seatbelt in place.

"Of course," Ranger said from the driver's seat.

"How's Anastasia?" Andi asked. Anastasia was his daughter. He'd thought for many years that she was dead, but he'd recently discovered that was all a lie. Now, the girl was back in his life, and Andi couldn't be more thrilled for him.

"Good. She's spending the weekend with Karen." Karen was the nanny who'd taken care of Anastasia during the years while Ranger thought the girl was dead. She'd become like a grandmother to the girl. "This will be my first time away from her since she came back into my life. But Anastasia insisted I go."

"She's spunky like that." Andi flashed him a smile.

"Yes, she is." Pride stretched through his voice.

Ranger had recently cut his scraggly hair and shaven his overgrown beard, leaving him looking like a new man. Plus, with his daughter now back in his life and Simmy by his side, he had a new bounce in his step.

As they pulled away from the condo complex, Andi glanced back and saw the crowd of reporters had grown. They'd probably be camped out near Duke's place for as long as possible, either until the condo manager kicked them out, the police came, or Duke showed up with a statement.

"Looks like a zoo out there." Simmy frowned at all the vans and cameras.

"You can say that again," Duke muttered.

"Hey, man." Ranger glanced back at Duke. "I'm sorry about all this."

"You're not the only one." Duke's voice sounded stiff.

Andi glanced at Duke's hand and saw he still gripped that note. No doubt his thoughts were racing through all the possibilities for truth—no matter how elusive it might be.

They filled their friends in on everything during the short drive to the Grayling Lodge, where they would be meeting.

The place was eclectic with local paintings filling much of the wall space and a stuffed bear in the corner. There was also a knight in shining armor, neon signs advertising aromatherapy steam rooms, and extravagantly gaudy lights that served as conversation pieces.

The place didn't look like much on the outside—like a cheap motel, really. But on the inside, it was a whole different story.

Staying here was an experience within itself.

Andi felt a rush of nerves as they stepped inside.

She was never one to back away from an argument. It was part of the reason she'd become an attorney. She didn't mind conflict.

But she cared about the members of the Arctic Circle Murder Club. They'd become like family to her over the past several months.

Seeing them broken up like they had been for the past few weeks had been difficult, to say the least.

They were doing a good thing together through the podcast and making a real impact. They somehow had to move beyond their differences.

Just as they reached the front doors, she saw a van pull into the parking lot.

A news van.

Her heart raced.

They needed to talk to Alfonzo. Ask him to keep reporters out.

Somehow, the media must have caught wind of the fact that Duke had a meeting here at the lodge.

And now everything was going to be a lot more difficult.

nine

AS SOON AS Andi saw Duke and Mariella regarding each other with a certain iciness, Andi knew she couldn't let it go.

They were in a conference room owner Alfonso Dominic let them use whenever they were here so they could have some privacy.

Alfonso was just as eccentric as the hotel itself. The man was tall and thin except for a protruding belly. Probably in his fifties, he had salt-and-pepper hair and a mustache that curled on the sides. He walked with a cane, and a monocle covered one eye.

They'd heard the man had made money in the oil business, and this hotel was a fun side project since he no longer had to work.

From the wary looks on everyone's faces, Andi knew they were going to need the privacy that room offered.

They all stood in a circle just inside the doorway, wasting no time getting to the heart of the matter.

Andi spoke first. "Listen, we need to get everything out in the open. No more beating around the bush or dirty looks or unspoken conversations. Let's just say what's on our minds and figure things out."

"I would *love* to get things out in the open." Mariella crossed her arms and glanced at Duke, her long, blonde waves falling halfway down her back and her pink outfit making her look deceptively like an airhead. "I'm not the monster you make me out to be."

Duke scowled. "Finding justice should be our first priority. Not publicity or social media likes or making Alpine happy. *Justice.* When we first came together, I thought we were all on the same page."

"Those are the things I want also!" Mariella continued to stare at him. "I only want open communication about it."

On the last case they'd worked as a team, Duke had spoken with a local reporter who'd shared information with him, in return for them sharing information with her. It had helped to break the case, but Mariella hadn't been happy. That information had been shared without discussing it as a team.

But Duke had claimed there was no time for discussion. He'd had to decide on the spot.

Mariella, however, didn't seem convinced.

"All I want is open communication," Mariella continued, an edge of hurt in her voice.

"I'm in favor of open communication." Duke's gaze remained stony.

"Great!" Andi waved her hands like an umpire declaring a play was safe. "It sounds like we all want the same thing then. Can we agree on that?"

She glanced back and forth between Duke and Mariella. After a moment of hesitation, the two of them nodded.

A touch of relief swept through her. "Okay then. Now that this is settled, we have other important things we need to talk about. We don't have any time to waste here. I know that you've all heard the news about Celeste."

They took their seats around the round table that had been set up in the room. Usually, there were mics and cameras on the table as well as a murder board nearby that Mariella blinged out with sparkles and all things pink.

Andi spotted the murder board on the other side of the room, but it hadn't been decorated yet in true Mariella fashion. All the equipment lay on a different table.

Clearly, Mariella hadn't been certain how this would turn out.

"I'm sorry to hear about Celeste," Mariella started with a glance at Duke. "I can only imagine what you're feeling right now."

Duke's expression remained stony. But he did pull out

the note he'd received from Celeste and put it on the table. "This was left outside my back door."

Everyone leaned closer to read it, and their reactions varied from surprised to hopeful to outraged.

"Maybe this will be your chance to get some resolution," Mariella said.

"I don't trust that note," Ranger said.

"Maybe Celeste thinks you're the only one who can help," Simmy started. "The only one who will believe her."

Matthew remained quiet, soaking everything in.

He was the techie of the group. Duke and Ranger had been teaching him some self-defense skills, but Matthew would most likely always be a desk jockey type.

And that was okay. Matthew was smart and resourceful and just fine the way he was.

According to Mariella, he was also talking to a girl online, and he seemed to be pretty happy with his life behind the computer.

"So I've been thinking about it." Andi tapped her pen on the table. "Thinking about how we could all proceed with this. Mariella, I know you will be busy with all the admin work for the podcast. I'm wondering if Matthew could trace the number of the phone call I got yesterday."

"The call you got yesterday?" Mariella questioned.

Andi snapped her head back, realizing she hadn't explained. She told everyone what had happened.

"I'd be happy to see what I can do," Matthew said.

"Ranger and Simmy, I'm hoping you can look into these people who died in California," Andi continued. "See if you can find out more information on them. Maybe find a link between them—if there is one."

"Of course," Ranger said.

She looked at Duke. "I'm hoping you and I can talk to Celeste's former coworkers at the hospital. I know you've talked to them before. But it's been two years, and it can't hurt to get their thoughts right now, given these new developments."

"We can do that." Duke's voice sounded a little friendlier but not quite normal still.

"I'd also like to talk to your neighbors and see if anybody saw anyone go into your backyard last night or early this morning," Andi finished. "Maybe somebody has a security camera that picked up something, and we can see who dropped off this note."

An unreadable look filled Duke's eyes as Andi added that last part.

He really wanted to believe this was Celeste, didn't he?

The thought made her heart go into a tailspin. Yet she couldn't blame him either.

Despite whatever he was feeling, he nodded. "Sounds like we have a lot to do."

"I guess it does." Andi looked back at the rest of the group. "We should probably get busy."

Just as she said those words, she looked up.

A man with dirty-blond hair peered in through the door, which was barely open.

How long had he been there listening?

As soon as he saw she'd noticed him, he took off in a run.

Andi rushed to her feet and chased after him.

———

DUKE SAW Andi rise and run toward the door.

Something was wrong.

Quickly, he stood and took off after her.

She paused in the hallway and glanced around.

"Andi?" He stopped beside her, noting her tense expression. "What's going on?"

"Some man with dirty-blond hair was eavesdropping. The fact he's running indicates he's guilty."

Eavesdropping? That didn't sound good.

"You go left, I'll go right," Duke murmured. "But stay safe."

As Andi took off in one direction, he headed in the opposite.

But he didn't see anybody suspicious down the hallway.

When he reached the door at the end, he shoved it open and ran outside, hoping to catch a glimpse of this mystery man.

He paused in the parking lot. That's when he heard a car engine rev.

Then a dark sedan squealed from the lot, heading toward the street. And the driver didn't even stop at the entrance. Instead, he bolted into traffic, narrowly missing a collision.

Duke tried to soak in any details he could about the vehicle.

However, the license plate was covered in mud. He couldn't read it.

He could only tell it was a dark, older-model sedan.

Not helpful.

He let out a sigh of frustration as he watched the vehicle disappear around the corner.

Then he headed back inside.

He and Andi met near the conference room, and he gave her the update on the car.

She frowned, clearly uneasy about the whole thing.

"You really think that guy was listening to us?" Duke asked.

"He could have been a reporter, for all I know." Frustration rose in her gaze. "I have no clue."

"We'll keep our eyes open in case he shows up again."

"So much has already gone wrong," Andi murmured. "I just don't want something else to be added to our plates."

"Me neither," Duke said. "Me neither."

ten

THINGS WERE GOING ACCORDING to plan.

This had been a long time in the making, and everything had to work just as I designed. One thing out of place could mean failure.

I couldn't let that happen.

I sat in my car outside the Grayling Lodge. Sunglasses stretched over my eyes, and a hat covered my head. No one should recognize me. My windows were tinted enough that it would be hard to see inside.

I knew the murder club was going to meet in that hotel room, which was why I'd had a listening device planted by their table. I wanted to hear what they were talking about and what they were going to do.

People were depending on me to succeed. I had to pull out all the stops.

I'd seen each group member go inside the building.

Now I watched as Duke and Andi emerged. I wondered where they were going.

I would find out. I would listen. I would trail them.

Meanwhile, I would also listen to everything being said inside the conference room. My earbuds were in and fully charged.

Multitasking at its finest.

If you would have asked me five years ago, I'd never thought I would be in this position. This hadn't been my plan.

Yet here I was. Desperate.

I couldn't fail.

These people were brilliant. I would use them, even if they didn't know it.

As they climbed into the SUV owned by Ranger, I started my car. I knew Duke was bright. Andi also.

I would need to be careful as I followed them.

But I could do it. I could be a ghost.

In fact, I'd become an expert at it.

eleven

AS SOON AS Duke climbed into Ranger's vehicle—his friend let them borrow it since Duke's was still at the condo—his phone rang.

Gibson's name popped up on the screen.

He'd figured the state trooper would check in with him today.

"Are you going to tell him about the note?" Andi asked before he answered.

"I . . . I don't know," Duke told her honestly. "I know full transparency is a good idea. But if I tell him, then Gibson will include the feds on this. They'll be watching everything."

"And Celeste might be spooked," Andi finished.

"Exactly." His chance to see her would be ruined.

He made up his mind right then as to what he would do.

He would keep quiet about the note. For now, at least.

He answered the phone and put it on speaker as he pulled away from the hotel.

"How's everything going this morning?" Gibson started.

"As well as can be expected," Duke said. "Any updates?"

"We've been questioning people at the university about William Ladak."

A few months ago, they discovered that Celeste had been chatting online with a man named William Ladak, also known as Bobby Lad. Professor Ladak had been teaching philosophy at the college level for years, including at the University of Nebraska. Celeste had lived there for about six months when she was a traveling nurse.

William had a squarish face, light brown hair, and broad shoulders. He disappeared the day after Duke spotted the blonde woman, possibly Celeste, with him. He'd also immediately resigned from the college.

"What do we know about him exactly?" Duke had told Gibson about the man earlier, but with this new evidence coming to light, maybe the police would dig deeper.

"Nothing much new, unfortunately," Gibson said. "His girlfriend did fit Celeste's description. But there's no indication where he went when he left the university. It's like he also just disappeared."

"So you're telling me that Celeste, as I knew her,

wasn't real and neither is this William guy?" Duke clarified, his grip on the steering wheel tightening.

"That's what it's looking like right now." Gibson paused as if trying to figure out how to word his next question. "Do you think what was between you and Celeste was real?"

"Of course." Duke's back muscles tightened. "What are you suggesting?"

Was he saying Celeste faked her relationship with him? Because nothing about the relationship had seemed fake. He'd looked into her eyes. Had seen the connection and affection there. You couldn't simulate that kind of thing.

Besides, what reason would Celeste have for faking a relationship with him? It wasn't as if Duke had anything that would benefit her.

Just the idea of it irritated him.

"I'm not suggesting anything," Gibson said. "I'm just asking questions."

"Do you think she was using me?" Duke turned toward the downtown area. "For what?"

"I'm just playing with various theories," Gibson said. "But I wondered if there were any cases you worked with the CID that Celeste might have wanted to find out more information on. Does that fit with anything you can think of? Were there any highly sensitive investigations that someone might want to get information from you about?"

He didn't even consider it. "No. Celeste would never do that. The thought is ridiculous."

However, there were cases. Hard cases. Cases that had changed his outlook on things.

Especially Operation No Name.

He shoved that thought aside. It wasn't as if Celeste had even known about it. He didn't discuss his work with her.

She'd had no clue what he was working on.

"Okay." Gibson's voice seemed to indicate he was taking a step back. "Like I said, I'm just asking questions."

"You're looking in the wrong direction."

Gibson didn't say anything a moment until finally, "Okay. But if you find out anything or remember anything, let me know."

Duke agreed.

He felt Andi's gaze boring into him as he ended the call.

Finally, he glanced at her.

"What?" The word came out, sharper than he intended.

She shrugged, clearly trying to be more nonchalant than she actually felt. "I'm just soaking everything in."

"You didn't know Celeste like I did." His jaw hardened as he said the words. "She wasn't the type to fake a relationship."

"I'm not saying she was."

As Duke glanced in his rearview mirror, he spotted a

car swerve out from behind the vehicle directly behind him.

The driver zigzagged, nearly hitting an oncoming driver in the opposite lane.

As the vehicle sped toward them, Duke sucked in a breath and braced himself.

———

ANDI GLANCED BEHIND HER.

Saw the car.

Then she grabbed the door handle on one side and the arm rest on the other.

That driver was coming right at them.

Vehicles around them honked and swerved to avoid a collision.

"What in the world?" Andi craned her neck to watch. "The driver isn't even trying to be subtle."

"No, he's not." His gaze slid to the rearview mirror again. "It's like he's lost his mind."

Duke jerked the wheel to the right and turned onto another street.

The other car followed.

Duke and Andi were definitely the target.

Duke pressed the accelerator, trying to get away.

Andi's heart pounded in her ears.

The driver sideswiped another vehicle in the oncoming lane.

The other car threw on brakes, a squeal filling the air.

Then the car smashed into a light pole.

No . . .

Andi wanted to turn around. To help the other driver.

But stopping right now could get them killed.

"What is this guy trying to do?" Andi murmured.

"Good question." Duke turned, a hard left this time.

Andi glanced behind her, holding her breath as she waited to see the driver's next move.

When she saw the man careening after them, she braced herself for the impact.

twelve

DUKE'S MUSCLES tightened as he glanced in his rearview mirror.

At any minute, that car was going to hit him.

The vehicle was going fast enough that it could do some damage.

He turned his attention back to the road in front of him.

Saw a line of cars had stopped at a nearby traffic light.

He had to figure out something.

If Duke didn't stop this guy, he would hit them. Then Duke would be propelled into all the vehicles in front of him.

Duke didn't want anyone to get hurt.

He let out a grunt as his knuckles turned white.

He headed toward the sidewalk in front of him. It was empty, and no one was in sight right now.

But instead of hitting the sidewalk itself, he turned at the last minute.

Andi gasped as the SUV spun around.

He watched the other driver as if in slow motion.

The man threw on brakes. Tried to turn.

But it was too late.

He rammed into a mailbox on the corner.

Duke let out a breath as he watched the car come to a stop.

Without hitting anything else.

"That was close," Andi muttered.

"Tell me about it."

Duke hopped from the car and ran toward the man. He could already hear the sirens in the distance.

Someone had called the cops.

Good.

He quickly observed the other driver. Blood ran down his forehead, and he appeared dazed.

"What were you thinking?" Duke demanded as he jerked the door open.

The man, probably in his forties and wearing a polo and khakis as if on his way to work, shook his head. "I . . . I don't know what happened."

"What do you mean you don't know what happened?" Duke couldn't keep the outrage from his voice.

"How did I even get here?" The man glanced around as if bewildered.

Duke shook his head. Was this guy on drugs or something?

The way he was talking, he sounded out of his mind.

Andi appeared beside him. She'd overheard the whole conversation, and the two of them exchanged a glance.

Before they could ask any more questions, the police pulled up and took over the scene.

———

ANDI AND DUKE remained at the scene for an hour as an officer took their statements.

Andi watched as medics checked over the driver of the other vehicle. It appeared he had some type of medical situation that had caused him to act erratically.

So maybe he really hadn't been targeting them.

Then why had it seemed as if he was following their every move?

It didn't make sense.

Andi was thankful no one else had been hurt. The driver of the car who had hit the light pole only had minor injuries. The paramedics would be taking him to the hospital for an evaluation as well.

Finally, she and Duke were freed to go.

They climbed back into Ranger's SUV. Once inside, Andi tucked her hands beneath her legs, trying to get the trembling to stop.

The adrenaline surge had caused the trembles and ratcheted up her heart rate.

Duke let out a deep breath as he cranked the engine. "That was unexpected."

"To say the least," Andi said. "We're about an hour behind now. We should get to the hospital. Continue with our plan."

"I agree." He put the SUV into gear and started down the road.

"So, is there anyone specific at the hospital you're going to talk to?"

Duke thrummed the steering wheel with his thumbs as if getting out nervous energy. "Yes, as a matter of fact, there is. As you know, Celeste was a traveling nurse. And she was good at her job. She was good at making relationships fairly quickly. She had one of those personalities."

Andi did *not* have that type of personality. She had the personality that often rubbed people the wrong way. But the friends she did have she was loyal to.

"The woman I want to talk to is Evelyn. She was the one friend Celeste talked about. They seemed to get along well and often had lunch together. Even did a few things on weekends."

"Was Evelyn also a traveling nurse?"

"No, but she hadn't been at Tanana Regional for very long either. The two of them bonded because of that also. They're about the same age, and Evelyn wasn't married either. I think she had a serious boyfriend, however.

Anyway, I talked to Evelyn several times after Celeste disappeared, wanting to know if she had heard anything. She hadn't, and she was concerned also."

"Then it sounds like she might be a good person to talk to."

"Let's hope so." They turned into the parking lot of the hospital. "Last I heard she was still working here. Hopefully that's still the case."

Duke paused after he pulled into a space, making no effort to get out.

"Andi . . . you've always been honest with me. What are you really thinking right now?" Duke turned to her, giving her his full attention. "Do you think Celeste was using me?"

Andi licked her lips. "I don't really know what to think. I'm just as confused as you are."

He nodded slowly. "Thank you. I want you to continue to be honest with me. I need someone who will tell me the truth. Someone to keep me grounded. Because my emotions are getting in the way right now."

"You can count on me."

He glanced at the hospital before grabbing the door handle. "Okay then. Let's get inside and see if we can find out anything."

thirteen

ANDI HAD BEEN honest when Duke asked her the question.

She really didn't know what to think.

On one hand, it was highly suspicious that Celeste and William Ladak both didn't truly exist. That they'd been living in Fairbanks together. That they'd been hiding out right under their noses after Celeste supposedly disappeared from Gates of the Arctic.

Duke had good instincts, and Andi found it hard to believe he'd be engaged to a woman who was just using him.

Still, she would give him time to think things through. Maybe some type of memory would trigger him and lead him to another conclusion.

For now, they were inside Tanana Regional Hospital and headed toward the information desk.

Andi didn't have any knowledge of who Celeste had worked with, but she trusted that Duke did.

Duke talked to the woman at the front desk, and then they headed to the fourth floor.

As soon as they stepped off the elevator, Duke strode toward a woman wearing pink scrubs standing by a computer at the nurses' station. She had honey-blonde hair cut into a pixie style. Her eyes lit with recognition when she saw him, and she turned from the computer.

"Duke McAllister . . ." Evelyn paused and placed her hands on her slim hips. "I kind of thought I might see you."

Her voice didn't sound especially excited, but there was an underlying warmth to it.

Evelyn's gaze slipped to Andi, and Andi saw the conclusions the woman instantly drew.

She assumed Andi and Duke were together.

"This is my friend Andi," Duke quickly said. "She's helping me look into what happened to Celeste."

Andi wasn't sure why those words disappointed her. What he said was true. But Duke was clearly trying to create distance between them.

It somehow felt like rejection.

"Nice to meet you." Evelyn nodded at Andi.

Duke shifted closer. "Listen, do you have a minute?"

She didn't hesitate. "For you? I've got two minutes. Follow me."

Andi swallowed hard, curious about what this woman might say.

———

BEING in the hospital caused memories to fill Duke.

He would often come here on his lunch break when Celeste was working. He'd bring her something to eat—usually a poke bowl from her favorite food truck. Then she'd regale him with stories of her workday, not disclosing any of her patients' names, but describing them in vivid detail anyway.

She had loved her job as a nurse. She loved people.

Which was another reason why Duke had a hard time envisioning her as a killer.

Evelyn led them into a small, empty waiting room and shut the door.

"I saw the news story." Evelyn shook her head, her expression tightening. "I can't believe it."

"Neither can I," Duke told her. "I'm . . . I guess you could say I've been in a bit of a tailspin ever since."

"I can only imagine." Evelyn let out a sigh. "I wish you could talk to Dr. Thirstman."

"Who's Dr. Thirstman?" Andi asked.

"She and Celeste really hit it off. They talked all the time. But the doctor is in Hawaii right now and won't be back until next week."

Duke vaguely remembered the name, though he hadn't realized Celeste was close with the doctor.

"The FBI has already been by here asking questions," Evelyn continued.

He wasn't surprised. "What did you tell them?"

Evelyn shrugged and rubbed her arm absently. "There wasn't much to tell them. I really liked Celeste. She was a good nurse. Her patients loved her. I never saw her doing anything that might potentially harm her patients. In fact, it was the opposite. She always went out of her way to make sure everyone was cared for, comfortable, and happy. The Celeste I knew would never do the things she's being accused of."

"That's what I think too." Evelyn's words brought Duke a certain measure of comfort—comfort he desperately wanted right now. "Did she ever mention to you that she'd worked in California?"

"She didn't." Evelyn paused before flinching. "Although there was this one time she slipped up. I didn't think much of it at the moment. I mean, we all say things and then correct ourselves, right? Especially after the end of a long shift."

Duke's spine straightened. "What did she say?"

"She said something about how even the hospitals in California were glamourous. Then she quickly explained that her friend who was also a traveling nurse had told her about a stint she did working in a Hollywood hospital. I wouldn't have questioned Celeste's words except I thought I saw a touch of guilt in her eyes."

Duke stored that information away.

It had just been a slip-up, right?

Just like her mention of Hollywood with him was a slip-up.

But if that were true, why did Duke feel like a seed of doubt had been planted and was starting to take root?

fourteen

"JUST BECAUSE CELESTE mentioned something about Hollywood to Evelyn doesn't mean Celeste actually lived in California," Andi murmured as she and Duke waited at the elevator after talking to Evelyn. "She could have just visited."

Duke pressed the button on the elevator again, harder this time. "But she slipped up with me also."

Andi swallowed hard. She'd been thinking about that but hesitated to say it aloud.

"Earlier, I assumed Celeste had misspoken when she was talking," Duke continued. "She quickly corrected herself. Now I'm thinking it wasn't a mistake after all. Celeste really was hiding something."

"Even if she lived or worked in California, that doesn't mean she actually killed those people."

Duke glowered. "I know. But I don't like this."

"I know everything inside you is screaming that you need to find out answers. But whatever Celeste did, even though you're connected, you're not truly a part of it. Even if she's guilty, it's not like you helped her with anything. The murders happened before you even met her."

"I know, but if she had one secret, there could be more." Duke clamped his mouth shut, unwilling to say anything else.

The elevator door opened, and they stepped inside.

Thankfully, they were the only ones there.

"I know if I tell you to forget about this that it won't work." Andi locked her gaze with his. "So I'm not going to tell you that. But you could just let this go."

"You're right, I can't do that."

Andi nodded. She knew he'd say that.

But it was true. He *did* have a personal stake in it.

She just hated to see him so worked up. She wanted to fix it.

But the only way to fix it was by finding answers.

They stepped off the elevator, and Andi paused.

Three police officers hurried past them.

She squinted. What was going on?

She glanced toward the front door, hoping to see something to give her answers.

Gibson stood there dressed in uniform, O'Brian beside him.

As soon as Gibson spotted Duke and Andi, he strode their way.

O'Brian gave them a look but hurried by as if on a mission.

Based on the tight set of Gibson's jaw, he had bad news.

"Gibson?" Duke stared at him, a touch of both exhaustion and caution in his voice.

"I don't know how to say this so I'm just going to cut to the chase." Gibson locked his gaze with Duke's. "Someone was murdered here at the hospital last night. Security footage shows . . . Celeste leaving the scene."

———

DUKE'S THOUGHTS rumbled in his head.

He couldn't have heard Gibson right.

But he knew he had.

His head pounded harder.

"So you think Celeste is in Fairbanks," Duke started. "That she came into this hospital recently, and that she killed someone right after accusations against her were made? What sense does that even make?"

Gibson's gaze darkened. "There's more. During the six months Celeste worked here, four patients died under mysterious circumstances."

Realization rolled over Duke. "You think Celeste killed them too?"

"I'm trying not to make any assumptions. But now that we know about what happened in California then, yes, that is a possibility. The FBI is investigating every place where she was employed and looking into any deaths that occurred during that time. Standard protocol."

"I understand," Duke murmured.

"We're trying to retrace her footsteps during the time she was a traveling nurse, but her different aliases make it difficult," Gibson continued. "We believe her real name is Kelly Hanson. We also believe she's used the named Ella Fisher and then Celeste Dawson, of course."

More questions pressed on him. "What about the person who died today? Why would Celeste kill him or her?"

"His name is James Parsons, and he was the hospital administrator. Last night, at our request, he began looking into some patients who died while under Kelly Hanson/Celeste Dawson's care. We believe Kelly found out about it and killed him in order to keep him silent. Then she destroyed several files. Parsons' assistant just got in—she came in late today—and she discovered him in his office, sprawled on the floor with a knife in his back."

Duke sucked in a breath, his head spinning. "Can I see the footage from the hospital?"

Gibson's expression tightened into a frown. "I'm sorry, but no. Not now, at least."

Duke remained quiet, thoughts roiling, before finally asking, "You said this happened last night?"

"That's right."

He pressed his eyes closed, dreading the fallout of this admission. But he couldn't stay quiet any longer. "There's something else you should know. Someone—maybe Celeste—left a note for me at my condo last night."

"What?" Gibson's voice turned sharp.

Duke opened his eyes again as he nodded. "It could be a fake, but the handwriting seems to match."

"Why didn't you tell me this earlier?"

"I should have. But I wanted to look into this first myself." Duke dipped his hand into his pocket, his fingers wrapping around the paper.

Gibson gave him a reprimanding look before asking, "Do you have this note with you?"

"I do." Duke pulled it from his pocket and handed it to him. Before he even asked, Duke explained what their secret spot was. Gibson jotted notes down as Duke spoke.

"We're going to need to have some agents present when you meet her."

"She'll know they're there and won't show up."

"We'll be subtle."

Duke said nothing. But he didn't like the idea. That was precisely why he hadn't wanted to tell the cops.

"We'll talk more about that later." Gibson shifted, his gaze narrowing in on them. "What are you two doing here?"

"I came here to talk to an old coworker of Celeste's,"

Duke told him. "To see if she remembered anything or learned anything new."

"Did she?"

"Not really." Duke's jaw muscle flinched at the admission. "I wasn't hoping for much, just closure I suppose."

Gibson's gaze latched onto his. "I hate to tell you this, but closure isn't something I think you're going to be getting anytime soon."

fifteen

AS ANDI and Duke remained in the lobby, she tried to process everything they'd just learned.

If Celeste was a killer, it only made sense that she might have carried on with her bad deeds here.

But a mercy killing, though wrong, was one thing.

Killing a hospital administrator in cold blood was an entirely different story.

She glanced near the gift shop and saw a figure dart away.

She squinted. Was she seeing things?

"Walk with me," she murmured to Duke.

"What's up?" He fell into step beside her.

"I thought I saw someone over here." She stepped into the gift shop and looked around. There was only a clerk behind the counter.

He'd almost looked like that man who'd been eavesdropping on them in the conference room. The one they suspected might be a reporter.

"Seeing things?" Duke asked.

"Maybe."

They turned to step back into the lobby and practically ran into a woman coming inside.

Based on her scrubs, the fortysomething woman was a nurse.

She took one look at Duke and recognition filled her gaze. "You! Your fiancée is the one who killed some of our patients!"

Duke's face went white. Instead of responding, he pushed past her.

Andi followed behind.

But the woman continued to yell insults. "How does it feel to know your fiancée is a killer?"

Andi couldn't take it any longer. "It's not like that. He had nothing to do with this."

"Prove it!"

Andi shook her head, trying to ignore everyone around who stared at them.

They quickly made their way outside before they could hear any more of the woman's insults.

"I'M SORRY, DUKE," Andi said once they were back in the SUV. "I know this is hard for you."

Duke appreciated her efforts to comfort him. But there was nothing anyone could say or do that would make him feel better right now.

Everything he thought he'd known about Celeste had been turned upside down, and he felt as if he'd spent the past two years chasing a ghost. What was real and what wasn't? Nothing made sense.

"I have no idea what end is up." He stared out the windshield, his jaw hard.

"Gibson said he saw her on that video."

Duke raked a hand through his hair. "I know. That only makes this even more confusing. I was trying to deny it, but why would Celeste come back to this area when everyone is looking for her? Why would she come to the hospital and murder someone? Why risk all that?"

"I say we go to your condo complex and talk to your neighbors. Maybe someone saw something that will help us."

"I was hoping you would say that." Duke put the SUV into Drive. "Because those are my thoughts exactly."

They pulled up to the complex only ten minutes later. Reporters had left the area, probably to head to the hospital. But he had no doubt they'd be back.

Several doors they knocked on didn't get answered. A couple of people were home but hadn't seen anything.

On the seventh unit, they hit the jackpot.

The woman had a security camera and offered to let them come inside.

The woman, Doris, was probably in her sixties, lanky and wrinkled with thinning, faded blonde hair that came to her butt. Her raspy voice indicated she was probably a smoker. Duke said he had never talked to her before, but Andi thought the woman seemed nice, albeit someone who might have lived a hard life.

Doris grabbed an electronic tablet, sat at the table, hit a few buttons, and then aimed the screen toward them. "It's a lot to look through. But I have two of those cameras outside that record everything, not just movement. I had a break-in last year, and my son installed them. One in the front and one in the back—that's where the burglars got in."

"Do you mind?" Duke pointed at the tablet. "I'm pretty good at these things."

"Not at all." She handed it to him.

Andi leaned closer as he scrolled through the footage.

Starting at 9:00 p.m., he began to fast forward. There was mostly nothing on the video except darkness and flying insects crossing the screen on occasion.

At midnight, a man and woman walked by, laughing as if they'd just come in from a long night of partying. Their arms were draped around each other in a way that showed they were crazy about each other.

A fox scurried across the yard around 2:00 a.m.

Then at 3:30, a figure appeared on the screen.

Duke slowed the footage to normal speed.

Then they watched.

The movement was so quick they almost missed it.

But someone wearing all black ran past, moving quickly as if they didn't want to be caught.

"Can you rewind?" Andi asked.

Duke rewound the footage, then played it in slow motion.

The video *definitely* showed a figure in black with something white in hand. Based on the build and shape, the visitor was a tall, thin woman. Her hair was mostly concealed by a black cap, but strands of blonde peeked out.

Then right before she slipped off the screen, the woman glanced at the camera as if realizing it was there.

Duke paused the footage.

Though it was grainy, Andi was sure of one thing.

The woman looked an awful lot like Celeste.

Just as he paused it, another figure appeared.

A man wearing all black.

He was creeping behind Celeste.

And, by all appearances, she had no idea the man was there.

sixteen

DUKE GOT a copy of the video. Then he and Andi headed back to the lodge to meet the rest of the team.

Maybe someone else had other news that would point them to answers.

Maybe.

But he couldn't stop thinking about that video and asking himself why.

If it was Celeste, *why* would she come back to Fairbanks right now while she was making national news?

It didn't make sense.

She would have to have a really good reason to risk it.

Had she really killed the hospital administrator here in Fairbanks? Had she killed those other patients who'd died via mysterious deaths while she worked here?

What about the six people in California? Were there even more victims they didn't know about?

Duke still couldn't believe it. He didn't care what anyone else said.

Celeste just wasn't capable of that.

The questions continued to circle in his head as he and Andi headed inside and met the rest of the team. They all sat at the round table together. Just as before, he was physically with the team. But mentally, he felt a million miles away.

"I'll start." Ranger rose from his seat, papers in hand. "Here are photos of all the people who died in Burbank."

Ranger spread the pictures on the table. On top of each photo, he placed an information sheet about each person.

"The feds believe the first victim was a man named Isaac Peters," Ranger started. "He was sixty-three and had MS."

He went through the rest of the victims.

Lorinna Buckley, fifty-three, inoperable brain tumor.

Jack Marshall, sixty-eight, Parkinson's.

Ivor Brackston, thirty-three, paraplegic after a car accident ten years earlier.

Staci Lockard, twenty-eight. No known health conditions.

"These *could* have all been mercy killings." Andi tapped her lips with her finger as she stared at the images. "I hate to say it, but it's true. It looks like each of these people had some type of life-altering issue. All of them except maybe this last one, Staci Lockard." She pointed to a picture of a young brunette. "But she could have had some disease that's not disclosed."

"That's true," Simmy said. "With HIPAA laws, a person's health information isn't public. Matthew and I can see if we can find out more about her."

"According to the news reports, the woman they're claiming was Celeste, first worked at Northwest Regional, where the first three victims died," Ranger continued. "Then she moved on to work at another hospital. The other three victims were discovered there. Unfortunately, a lot of the pieces fit, and the picture that forms is one that makes Kelly/Celeste appear guilty."

Silence stretched as they all comprehended his statement.

Finally, Andi turned to Matthew, another question clearly on her mind. "Did you trace the number from that phone call to me last night?"

"I tried, but I couldn't. Probably a burner."

Andi nodded. "I figured as much."

Part of Duke didn't need to hear a definite answer from Matthew.

Because, proof or no proof, Duke firmly believed the caller had been Celeste.

———

"MAYBE WE SHOULD all grab a bite to eat," Andi suggested after several minutes of staring at the photos.

"It'll help us clear our minds."

She glanced around, waiting for everyone else's reaction.

No one seemed super excited about eating, but no one argued either. Maybe because they were out of ideas. There was no clear path forward on how to find answers. Sure, they could talk to the families of the victims, but they probably didn't know much. People Kelly/Celeste worked with probably wouldn't want to talk.

It left them at a standstill.

They headed to the restaurant next door, Grayling's Waterfront Restaurant and Pub. They ate at the place often when they were at the lodge for their monthly meetings. It was conveniently located only steps away from the lodge, connected by a deck that had a great view of the river stretching behind the property.

The waitress recognized them when they stepped inside the dimly lit place and directed them to their normal seats at a corner booth. The scent of seafood and beer surrounded them.

Andi waited until everyone had ordered before feebly asking, "Anyone else have any updates?"

She didn't have high hopes.

"Alpine called." Mariella's voice sounded tight, as if she were bracing herself for a confrontation by bringing up his name. "He asked about Steven Calderson, the inmate we're supposed to be looking into. I didn't know what to tell him."

Andi took a sip of her water, buying a moment.

Since they weren't supposed to be keeping secrets from each other, it was good Mariella had brought the subject up now.

"I need to interview witnesses." Andi set her drink down. "Considering what's happening now with Celeste, I figured it could wait."

"Alpine is very persistent that we look into this," Mariella continued before shrugging. "He feels strongly that an innocent man is on death row."

Irritation pinched at Andi's spine, but she forced herself to nod. "I understand. I'm doing my best."

Mariella nodded, but a war seemed to rage in her gaze. Just how much pressure was Alpine putting on her? And why? Why was this case so important to him?

And should he really be allowed to call the shots? That wasn't what they agreed to.

"Now, maybe we can talk about Celeste again." Andi turned to Duke. "I was wondering, did Celeste ever talk about her family? Maybe we could contact them."

Duke's face tightened. "She said she was an only child. Said her parents died when she was in college. At the time, it seemed tragic, but I didn't doubt what she said. I had no reason to."

Matthew cleared his throat. "I happened to do some research on Kelly Hanson. It turns out her parents are dead, and she was an only child." Matthew shrugged self-consciously before looking at Duke. "Sorry that doesn't help much."

Andi saw the emotions swirling in Duke's gaze.

Matthew's statement was another confirmation that this woman could be Celeste.

Andi tried to find the right words to say.

Before she could, movement in the restaurant's parking lot caught her eye.

She sucked in a breath as she watched two men walking toward the place.

It was those thugs from last night, the ones she'd been trapped in the van with.

They were here, and they appeared to be looking for someone.

She could only guess they were looking for her.

seventeen

ANDI JOLTED to her feet and glanced at her team. "If anyone asks about me, you haven't seen me."

"What?" Mariella muttered, her eyes narrowed with confusion.

"Duke can explain. I don't have time." Andi took off toward the back of the restaurant. She slipped inside the women's bathroom, into a stall, and locked the door.

Then she waited.

Bathrooms were never the best hiding spot. These guys were dangerous so they wouldn't be shy about going into a space marked for women only.

If she had thought things through a little more then maybe she could have slipped into the kitchen and out the back.

But right now, she was stuck here.

So she prayed for the best.

How had those guys found her? Andi knew for certain they hadn't seen her last night. If they had, they would have hurt her on the spot.

They must have checked some video footage at the warehouse where she'd left her car. They must know she'd seen what was in the back of the van. Now they'd come to silence her.

Her heart continued to thump into her chest as she waited. She glanced around the stall, which was fairly clean but nothing fancy. The bathroom probably hadn't been updated in at least twenty years.

Beige dividers. Beige toilet. Tiny blue square tiles on the floor with dark grout. A few names had been carved into the walls, but they looked to have been repainted multiple times over the years.

She continued to wait. In her haste to leave, she'd left her phone on the table. Now she couldn't even text her friends to ask them what they were seeing.

The door squeaked open, and her throat tightened.

Was it one of the men?

A tremble raked through her.

Carefully, she stood on the toilet so no one would see her feet if they glanced beneath the doors.

Then she waited for whatever would happen next.

———

DUKE WATCHED as the men entered the restaurant and glanced around. Even though the hostess talked to them, asking if they wanted a seat, the men scanned the place, appearing as if they didn't hear her.

"What is going on?" Mariella sounded bewildered as she looked from where Andi disappeared back to the rest of the group.

Duke glanced beside him and saw Andi's phone on the table. She must have accidentally left it.

Those men had her seriously rattled.

"Duke?" Mariella repeated.

Amidst the sounds of Tom Petty's "I Won't Back Down" playing on the overhead, Duke dragged his gaze to meet Mariella's. "It's a long story, and I'm not sure I even know all the details. But Andi ended up in the back of a van those guys were driving. They returned sooner than she expected, leaving her stuck there. They drove to some type of abandoned building in the middle of nowhere, and Andi texted me to help."

Ranger narrowed his gaze. "When was that?"

Duke's gaze continued to trail the men as they weaved past tables. "Last night. I managed to get her away without those guys seeing her. But clearly, they somehow learned she was back there."

Duke would have to figure that one out later.

For now, he didn't want to make any moves.

Then he remembered he was recognizable. He'd talked to those guys. If they put two and two together . . .

Duke turned to Matthew. "I need your hat. I don't want them to see me."

Before Matthew could contemplate it, Duke snatched the UCLA hat off his friend's head and pulled it down low over his own face.

Duke angled his back toward the men so they wouldn't get a good look at him. Then he continued to watch as they slowly made their way around the restaurant, searching all the faces.

A private dining area and party room were located around the corner. He watched the thugs head out of sight in that direction.

As far as Duke remembered, there were three doors down the hallway where Andi had disappeared. The men's restroom, the women's restroom, and the door to the kitchen.

Tension thrummed inside him as he watched and waited.

The men reappeared a few minutes later.

They were still searching for her.

They must have caught wind that Andi had been here. But how? Something had happened to alert them.

Had they tapped into the security cameras? Had another customer spotted her band reported her to these guys?

Duke didn't know. They'd need to figure that out later.

As the thugs began walking toward the bathrooms, Duke's muscles bristled.

He needed to stop them before they went inside.

Which meant things might get really ugly right now.

eighteen

ANDI HEARD someone step into the bathroom.

Unseen hands seemed to squeeze her throat until she couldn't breathe. All she could do was listen to the *thump, thump, thump* of her heart.

She glanced around, looking for something to defend herself with.

She supposed she could take the back off the toilet. It was ceramic and heavy. That might take out one of the guys. But what about the other one?

Her thoughts continued to race as she tried to put together a plan.

But she had nothing else on her. Nothing she could use to defend herself.

She heard a footstep. Then another. And another.

Whoever it was, they were now fully inside the bathroom. Walking toward the stalls if Andi gauged the sounds correctly.

A shadow hovered outside her stall door.

Andi held her breath. Waited. Tried to figure out what this person's next move might be.

Had one guy stationed himself outside the door as lookout while the other guy came after her?

A sick feeling roiled in her stomach.

Then she heard someone pushing at her door.

———

DUKE AND RANGER EXCHANGED A GLANCE. Then they both rose from the booth where they were seated.

They headed toward the hallway where the restrooms were. But just as they reached it, they saw the men disappear inside the men's room.

They could go in there after them.

But something told Duke to wait.

He motioned to Ranger, who nodded, and they slipped behind the wall and out of sight.

A few minutes later, the thugs emerged.

Again, Duke braced himself for whatever might play out.

Instead of going to the women's restroom, they turned to head back toward the front door.

Duke and Ranger hurried back to the dining area and took their seats, trying to look inconspicuous.

Duke kept one eye on the thugs as they headed out of the restaurant.

Relief swept through him.

But he didn't want to let this opportunity pass.

"Mariella, stay here for now." He turned to Ranger. "Can you check on Andi? I'm going to tail these guys and see what they're up to."

"I'm on it," Ranger muttered.

Duke rose, trying to stay a safe distance behind the men.

But he needed to figure out who these men were and what they wanted.

nineteen

ANDI HELD HER BREATH.

Then she heard the door next to her stall open. Close. Lock.

Then someone began whistling.

Was it strange that she thought it was a woman whistling? Could a person tell by a whistle if it was a man or a woman?

Andi couldn't be sure.

She carefully climbed off the toilet seat and leaned down.

A pair of women's tennis shoes appeared in the stall beside her.

It wasn't those men after all.

Her breath left her lungs in a whoosh.

She wasn't sure where those guys had gone, but they weren't in here.

Quietly, she unlocked the stall and tiptoed to the bathroom door. She cracked it open and peered out.

Ranger waited for her. "They're gone."

Even more relief swept through her.

She slipped out but stayed close to Ranger as they walked back into the dining area.

"Where did they go?" She glanced around, still not ready to completely let her guard down.

"Outside," Ranger said. "Duke's following them."

Her heartbeat ratcheted faster.

The last thing she wanted was for Duke to get in the middle of this.

He was good at lying low. Most likely, he would remain unseen.

But Andi still didn't want him to get hurt.

She started toward the door when Ranger grabbed her arm. "It's better if you stay here. Those guys are probably looking for you."

"But Duke . . ." She glanced at the door.

"I'll make sure he's okay. You stay put." Ranger's deep, rumbling voice didn't leave any room for argument.

Andi nodded before slowly walking back to the booth, her eyes on Ranger the whole time.

She prayed both he and Duke remained safe and that those men didn't decide to double back and check out the restaurant a second time.

———

DUKE REMAINED a careful distance behind the men. They'd driven that same black van to the restaurant, the one without windows in the back.

The one Andi had stowed away in.

He kept his head low, not wanting to draw any attention to himself. But that would be hard out here if he wanted to eavesdrop.

Instead, he pulled out his cell phone and paced near the restaurant as if making a call.

As he paused, he barely heard the two men talking near that van.

"She was supposed to be here," Missing Tooth said.

"Well, I didn't see her."

"Boss isn't going to be happy."

"Not going to be happy?" the second guy said. "He's not the one I'm worried about. It's you and me. He said he'd kill us if we didn't come back with her."

Duke's throat went dry.

These guys didn't want to kill Andi. They'd been instructed to bring her in. He didn't want to think about what they would do with her then.

His hand fisted.

He glanced up and saw Ranger heading his way but shook his head.

His friend paused and went back into the restaurant.

Duke muttered a few more things into his phone and leaned against the restaurant as if taking a business call.

"Where are we going to look next?" Missing Tooth asked.

"We need to keep scouting out the area. Fairbanks isn't a big town. We'll find her."

Part of Duke wanted to march right over there. To demand answers.

But he knew those men had guns, and they probably wouldn't be afraid to draw them.

For that reason, he remained where he was.

He needed to warn Andi . . . and keep an eye on her.

twenty

ANDI STOOD AS SOON as Duke stepped back inside the restaurant. She could hardly breathe as she waited to hear his update.

He strode to the booth, and they both sat down.

His eyes locked onto hers, a dead serious look permeating his gaze. "Those guys are looking for you. Someone gave them instructions to bring you to them."

"Victor . . ." Andi rubbed her arms as she felt a sudden chill.

"How in the world did they find out you were in the van?" Duke asked. "It doesn't make sense. They were clueless when I talked to them."

She nibbled on her bottom lip as she thought it through. "I wish I knew. The only thing I can figure is that maybe they checked the security cameras downtown where I parked near the van."

"Why would they watch that video?" Mariella asked. "Especially if everything was still in the back?"

"They're paranoid maybe." Andi shrugged. "Or maybe they were checking for something else and just happened to see me. These guys . . . they were meeting with one of Victor's men, but they beat that guy up pretty good. Maybe he called the police. It's hard to say."

"Maybe they noticed everything wasn't as they left it in the back of the van, so they decided to do some digging." Duke gave her a pointed look.

Andi shook her head skeptically. "I don't know. Have you seen those guys? They don't exactly seem detail-oriented. Believe me, the back of the van was not that neat when I climbed inside."

Duke's assessing gaze fell on her again. "I still don't understand why you got in that van in the first place."

Andi let out another sigh. "I was tailing one of Victor's men. He works at the office building here in Fairbanks."

"It wasn't the hitman, was it?" Mariella asked.

"No, I haven't seen him in a while." Andi shook her head, trying to stay focused. "Anyway, this guy makes lots of trips up to the oil fields. That's why I thought he might have something to do with Prometheus."

Prometheus was what Victor called a top-secret project he was working on.

"I followed this guy, hoping to get some answers," Andi continued. "He met with these two men behind a warehouse. I stayed back at first. Then the two men went to the man's car. While they did that, I decided to check out the van."

"And?" Duke continued to eye her.

"Just when I climbed into the van, I heard them return. They beat the man up and then took off. I didn't have time to get out."

"Did you find any answers?" Mariella asked, her gaze less judgmental than Duke's.

Andi frowned. "Not really. Except that there was a lot of money, several guns, weird little metal discs, and some random photos. I still don't know what they plan on doing with any of that stuff or where they got it, but I would bet it was all through illegal means."

"I don't know what to say about the guns and metal discs," Duke started. "But I know Victor has hefty bank accounts—probably even some hidden bank accounts. Why does he need his guys to drive around with wads of cash?"

Andi shrugged. "That's an excellent question, and I don't really know the answer."

"So you're in the back of this van, and they take off." Ranger crossed his meaty arms as he listened to the conversation. "What happened next? Where did these guys go, and how did you get away?"

"I texted Duke, of course." Andi cast a glance his way. "I sent him my location, and he pulled up right as the van came to a stop. He made up some story about being lost, which gave me the chance to slip away. He picked me up farther down the road."

"It was an abandoned building about twenty minutes north of Fairbanks," Duke said. "Honestly, I hardly looked at it. All I could think about was getting Andi far away from those men. They looked like trouble."

"I didn't get a good look at their faces either," Andi said. "It was more important that I get away than for me to see who they were meeting with, am I right?"

"Absolutely," Simmy said with a motherly nod.

Ranger let out a long sigh before shaking his head. "I don't know what's going on. It's going to take some more digging to find out those answers. Let us know what we can do to help you."

Andi nodded, gratitude filling her.

But before they could talk about it anymore, the TV above the bar caught her eye.

It was another story on Celeste, aka Kelly Hanson. This time, it was the local news, however.

"Hey, everyone . . ." Andi nodded toward the screen.

They turned to listen to the latest update.

But Andi had a sinking feeling in her stomach as she anticipated what might be said.

PART OF DUKE didn't want to hear an update.

But, like a bad accident, he couldn't look away. He

needed to know what the investigative journalists knew. What the latest update was.

As the group quieted at the table, Duke heard some of the report and read the rest in closed captioning at the bottom of the screen.

"We have some new developments on Nursy Mercy," the reporter said. "The woman supposedly killed six terminally ill patients in California four years ago. Now, she may have also killed five people at a Fairbanks hospital."

Everyone in the restaurant seemed to quiet and listen to the newscast.

"Four of the killings happened two years ago when she worked at Tanana Regional," the reporter said. "The most recent victim was hospital administrator, James Parsons, who may have caught on to what she was doing. Kelly Hanson, who later went by Celeste Dawson, hasn't been seen in two years since she disappeared while hiking at Alaska's Gates of the Arctic National Park."

The video cut from a photo of Celeste to . . .

Duke.

His throat tightened as his picture appeared on the screen, followed by a video of him walking to his condo. Based on his clothing, it had been taken yesterday. He hadn't even noticed a reporter had lurked nearby.

"No . . ." Andi murmured.

"While living in Fairbanks, Hanson was engaged to a man named Duke McAllister," the reporter continued.

"McAllister is now a tour guide here in Alaska. Police and federal agents have been seen talking to him about this case. His connection to Nursy Mercy has left authorities asking whether or not he might be involved."

O'Brian appeared on the screen. "We believe Ms. Hanson wasn't working alone when she killed her victims. The nature of what she did required help from someone else. For that reason, we're now looking into who might have been her accomplice."

Him, Duke realized. They were wondering if Kelly/Celeste's accomplice was Duke—at least during the time while she was here in Fairbanks.

The blood drained from his face until everything went still around him.

The story switched to the weather.

But he felt everyone's eyes on him.

The last thing he'd wanted was for his face to be on TV—for more than one reason.

But it was too late now. The story had already run.

Even worse, it was already past 1:00. That story had probably aired the first time at noon. News was already spreading throughout town.

Talk about irresponsible journalism . . .

A story like that could affect so many things, not just for Duke but for the people around him.

As if on cue, his phone rang.

It was Ericson, one of the tour guides who worked for him.

Duke muttered "excuse me" before putting the phone to his ear.

"Duke, we have a situation down here at the office." Ericson's normally friendly voice sounded stiff and tense. "You're going to want to get here ASAP."

"What's going on?" Duke's shoulders were already tense and achy as various scenarios shot through his head.

"A woman's here. She says your fiancée murdered her husband at Tanana General Hospital. Now she's demanding justice." Ericson paused as his voice cracked. "Duke . . . she's got a gun and is holding us hostage. She insisted I call you."

twenty-one

ANDI WATCHED as Duke rose from his seat. "I've got to go."

"What's wrong?"

"The wife of one of Nursy Mercy's Fairbanks victims is at my office, holding hostages. She wants revenge on me. I've got to go make this right."

Andi stood also. "I'm going with you."

He didn't seem to hear her as he continued toward the door.

Andi looked back at the rest of the crew and dropped a twenty on the table. "Sorry to run. But if you could look into those victims here at Tanana Hospital, that would be great. I'll keep you all updated the best I can."

Then she ran after Duke, knowing he'd leave without her if she lagged behind too much.

He was already in the SUV when she got there and

climbed in beside him. Mere seconds later, they pulled out of the lot and started down the road.

She quickly scanned everything around her, trying to make sure those two thugs from earlier were gone. She didn't see them anywhere. But she needed to remain on guard, just in case.

"Did you get any other details?" Andi asked.

Duke shook his head, his gaze intense as he drove a little too quickly. "No. But it sounds like a serious hostage situation."

Was all this because his picture and name had been leaked to the news? Most likely.

Andi hadn't even seen any reporters taking a video of him. But there clearly had been someone.

Maybe the man from earlier? Had he been a reporter? Maybe.

Andi knew Duke wasn't in the mood to talk, so she stayed quiet on the drive and let him sort out his thoughts.

Only moments later, they pulled up to the office building Alaska Arctic Tours was based out of.

Andi often helped him as a tour guide, so she'd been to the white office with the blue sign out front many times before.

Right now, police cars, some unmarked sedans, and a mobile crisis command center were parked haphazardly around it. News vans pulled in behind them.

Andi's gaze traveled to a man in a suit who held a phone as he faced the front window of Duke's building.

The man in charge? That was what Andi would guess.

She didn't want to picture the scene inside. But it was hard not to, everything considered.

Duke threw his SUV into Park and rushed toward the building. Andi quickly followed.

Gibson appeared, his arm jutting out to stop Duke before he got any closer. "You can't go in."

Duke's jaw hardened, and he stared at his building. "That woman wants me. I need to talk to her."

"She has a gun. A tourist is being held at gunpoint. Your employee Ericson is also in there."

The color drained from Duke's face.

"Who is this woman?" Andi asked.

"Her name is Ruby Logan. She's thirty-five. No prior record. Her husband, Dustin, had cancer, and he passed away at the hospital. They thought it was because of the disease." Gibson paused. "Until yesterday."

Duke's gaze remained on the building. "Who's the tourist?"

"A woman named Cyndee Waylen, who came in by herself to inquire about a tour while her family was napping after a long flight from Florida."

"Let me see if Ruby will trade her hostages for me." Duke's gaze locked on Gibson's. "Please. This is my battle, not theirs."

"That's not a good idea. Woodhaven, the guy in charge"—Gibson nodded toward the man in the suit—"will never go for that. We're trying to negotiate now."

"Then negotiate using me. Let me be the bargaining chip." Duke jammed his finger into his own chest.

Andi held her breath as she waited to hear what would play out.

Before anyone could decide, a commotion sounded from inside the office. Shouting. A crash. More yelling.

Nausea roiled in her gut as she imagined what might be going on inside.

She prayed everyone would get through this unscathed.

———

DUKE STARTED to run toward his office when Gibson grabbed his arm. "I can't let you do that."

"Please." He turned back to the officer, his gaze hard. "Let me talk to her."

Gibson glanced at Woodhaven.

Gibson and this man seemed to have some type of silent conversation.

"I can't put a civilian at risk," Woodhaven said.

"I'm hardly a civilian. I'm former CID. This is my business."

Woodhaven hesitated another moment before saying, "There are no guarantees as to what will happen."

"I know."

Woodhaven stared at him another moment before nodding.

Gibson released his grip on Duke's arm. "Fine. But we've got to do it our way, not yours."

"Whatever you say." Duke shrugged, trying to relax his shoulders. But it was no use.

Woodhaven nodded to another man. The next instant, they placed a bulletproof vest on him.

As the straps were tightened across Duke's chest, Woodhaven raised his phone, put it on speaker, and said, "Ruby, this is Jimmy Woodhaven again. Duke McAllister is here. He would like to trade himself for the woman and Ericson."

Silence, then Ruby said, "Duke McAllister needs to come inside first. Then I'll let the others go."

The woman's voice sounded thin and cracked with every other word. She was on the verge of having a total breakdown, wasn't she? And she was nowhere close to making a rational decision.

"We need your assurance that you won't hurt Cyndee or Ericson," Woodhaven said.

"I won't." Her voice hardened. "I only want Duke."

Andi looked up at Duke, not hiding the worry in her eyes. "This is a bad idea. What if she shoots you? She sounds like she's out of her mind. People don't act rationally in situations like this."

His heart thudded with another moment of regret. Not for himself. But he hated to see Andi so anxious. Yet he knew he couldn't live with himself if someone innocent was hurt because of him.

Although, if he were to examine the situation more closely, he'd have to admit he too was innocent.

If Celeste was the mastermind behind any of this, then Duke was as much of a victim as anyone else.

Yet another part of him refused to let him think of himself that way.

"Andi, it's going to be okay." He prayed that his words were true.

She continued to stare at him, her eyes wells of emotion.

Duke wished he could wipe away all her fear, sadness, and worry.

Right now, he had to save two innocent lives.

Duke reached out and squeezed Andi's hand.

Then he stepped away from her and squared his shoulders.

It was time for him to go in.

twenty-two

ANDI COULD HARDLY BREATHE AS she watched Duke walk toward that building.

More than anything she wanted to beg him to stay. To explain that they still had more conversations to be had. Whether he ended up with Celeste or her . . . whether he was still in love with Celeste or if he was in love with Andi . . .

At this very moment, it didn't matter. All that mattered was knowing he was okay. Once he got inside . . . there would be no one to help him.

Tears pressed at Andi's eyes before she could stop them.

She sucked in a deep breath, trying to get herself under control.

This was no time to get emotional. She had to stay calm.

She continued to hold her breath as Duke disappeared inside.

What would happen? What kind of conversation would he have with this woman?

Andi had been in that office so many times before. She could easily picture everything playing out. Duke's calm voice. His pleas for her to release the hostages.

But what she couldn't so easily picture was the outcome.

Would Ruby keep her end of the bargain?

Duke had worked as a detective with the Army CID, and he'd served many years before that as a soldier. He could handle himself in these situations.

But not many people could handle themselves around somebody who was crazy with grief.

Andi's eyes widened when she saw a shadow move near the door.

When nothing else happened, she wondered if she'd imagined the movement.

It was too quiet in there.

She practically held her breath as she waited.

Andi hated not knowing what was going on inside.

What would the woman do next?

———

DUKE STARED at the woman in front of him.

She had bright red hair, cut short and tight on the sides. Her skin looked pale and pasty.

Ruby Logan.

Right now, she'd come unhinged.

She gripped Cyndee by the bicep. Cyndee, a woman in her sixties with honey-blonde hair and a slight build, looked paralyzed with fear.

Ericson, a history major fresh out of college, stood near the desk, his breathing so shallow that Duke feared his employee might pass out. He tried to give the young man a reassuring look.

Then he turned back to Ruby.

He swallowed hard, knowing the situation was touchy.

Ruby held her gun in trembling hands and pointed it at Duke.

"You knew what she was doing, didn't you? You protected her. It's your fault." Her voice quivered as she said the words.

"I didn't know anything. I still don't. I don't believe my former fiancée did this." Duke raised his hands, trying to keep her calm.

Former fiancée? It was the first time Duke had ever referred to Celeste like that.

"The cops think she did it. I think so too." Spittle flew from Ruby's mouth as she said the words.

"Even if she did, I didn't have anything to do with it,"

Duke tried to reassure her. "I would never support murder. I'm the one who likes to bring people who hurt other people to justice."

Ruby stared at him, and Duke couldn't tell if she believed him or not.

"Someone needs to pay," she finally said, her nostrils flaring.

Duke raised his hands in the air. "I understand your desire for vengeance. I really do. What happened to your husband was a tragedy. Someone should pay. I'm trying to help the police right now to figure out answers. I'm the only one who knows certain things about Celeste. And I want to help them find her. But if you pull that trigger and kill me . . . then I can't help them."

Her eyes widened. "How do I know that what you're saying is true?"

A tear rolled down her cheek.

"I have no reason to lie. I haven't seen Celeste in two years. She dumped me and left me heartbroken. Now all these horrible things are coming to light. If it turns out that she is guilty . . . I'm not going to defend her actions."

"My husband is dead." Tears began to stream down her face.

Compassion tightened Duke's throat as he realized her pain.

"I know," Duke said softly. "I know."

Maybe he was reaching her, getting through, breaking down her walls.

But just as that thought entered his mind, her eyes narrowed, and she raised the gun.

"Someone needs to pay!" In the next instant, she pulled the trigger.

twenty-three

ANDI MUFFLED a scream when she heard the gunfire inside the building. Her hand flew over her mouth as she stared at the office.

Duke...

What if he had been shot?

Her heart raced as panic filled her.

No, not Duke...

The cops around her began to scurry, to get in place to breach the building.

Then Woodhaven began speaking into the phone.

He'd gotten through to Ruby, hadn't he?

Her breath caught.

Was it Ruby?

He put it on speaker, and Andi edged closer.

"Ruby, I need you to talk to us," Woodhaven said. "What just happened? Is anyone hurt?"

There was no response.

"Was anyone hurt, Ruby?"

Still nothing.

Woodhaven muttered something beneath his breath, his gaze clouding with anger.

Andi stepped closer to Woodhaven, knowing she could help. "I realize you don't know me, but can I try to talk to her?"

He stared at her, his eyes narrowed and looking at her as if she'd lost her mind. "I'm not sure that's a good idea."

"Look, I know it's unconventional," Andi explained. "But I was an attorney for a long time. Negotiating is my specialty—negotiating and convincing people to see things my way. Plus, I already did my research on Ruby's husband. I promise, I won't mess this up."

As she said the words, pressure mounted between her shoulders.

What had she just promised? And what if she *did* mess this up?

"She's legit," Gibson confirmed.

Woodhaven stared at her another moment before handing her the phone.

Andi licked her lips as she prepared herself to speak. She ignored the moisture that had formed on her hands.

"Ruby, are you there?" she started. "My name is Andi. I'm not a cop. I just want to talk to you."

There was no response.

"Ruby, I need to know that everyone inside is okay,"

Andi said. "Can you tell me that? You know that awful feeling you experienced when your husband died? We're all experiencing that out here right now as we wonder what happened inside. As we wonder if someone's hurt and if they need help."

Still no response.

Woodhaven raised his eyebrows at her, looking ready to grab the phone at any minute. Andi needed just a little more time.

"Ruby, I know you're not a bad person," Andi continued. "You're just hurting because of your husband's death. Your hurt is causing you to want to hurt other people, am I right? But that's not going to bring Dustin back. Nothing will. I read about your husband. He was a teacher and a good man. What do you think he's going to think about all of this?"

Silence passed for another moment, followed by her cry.

Andi's heart thumped harder. Maybe she was getting through to the woman after all.

"Can you tell me if everybody is okay?" Andi asked.

"They're fine," a quivering voice said on the other end. "I accidentally pulled the trigger. Nobody was hit."

"Good." Some of the stress flushed through Andi's body in one sweeping motion. "I'm so glad to hear that. Ruby, I think you know what you're doing is wrong. Why don't you let everyone go before you make the situation worse?"

Andi held her breath as she waited to hear what Ruby would say.

———

DUKE LISTENED to Andi on the other end of the phone.

He hoped she knew what she was doing.

So far, she'd been very convincing.

As he glanced at Ruby, he saw her shoulders drooping. The resolve leaving her gaze.

Her walls were coming down, and the woman was second-guessing herself, he realized.

Andi might just have a new career ahead of her as a hostage negotiator.

"Dustin wouldn't want this," Andi said again. "You know he wouldn't. He was a good man. And you know what? He's always going to live in your heart. I believe he's with us now. That he's watching you. I even believe that maybe he's trying to tell you to stop this."

Duke didn't think Andi believed that. But her words were reaching Ruby. He could see it in Ruby's gaze.

"Can you put the gun down?" Andi asked.

Duke stared at Ruby, waiting for what she would do.

The last thing he wanted was for her to accidentally pull that trigger again. Because next time, they may not be as lucky. Next time, she might actually hit someone.

Then another tragedy would be added upon what was already a string of other tragedies and crimes.

"If you turn yourself in, we can get you the help you need," Andi continued. "What you need is for someone to listen to you. To hug you. To hold you. To tell you that everything is going to be okay. I know this is really hard. You don't think anyone understands you. But there are people out there who've been through similar heartaches. They can help. They want to help."

"No one understands."

"One of my friends was murdered, Ruby. At first, I wanted to do just what you're doing. Then I decided there was a better way."

Duke's throat tightened at Andi's words.

"What's that?" Ruby asked, her attention on the conversation.

"I decided to make sure the killer gets justice the right way. I won't give up until he does. But I'm also not going to spend the rest of my life behind bars because of him. Then it will just be like he's winning all over again. Don't let the person who did this to your husband win again, Ruby. I promise you you'll regret it."

More tears rolled down Ruby's cheeks.

"Won't you put the gun down?" Andi continued. "Please? For your husband's sake?"

Those last words seemed to get to Ruby. Her arms loosened, and she began to lower the gun.

This was his opportunity.

Duke stepped closer and slipped the gun out of her hands.

"It's okay," he murmured.

He tucked the weapon into the back of his waistband. Then, before Ruby crumpled to the floor in a heap, he wrapped his arms around her in a hug and took the phone.

"She surrendered the gun," he said into the cell. "Everyone is okay."

He ended the call and put the phone on the floor.

As he did, officers flooded inside.

They surrounded Ruby and cuffed her. Then they rushed toward Cyndee and Ericson to check on them.

Duke released the tension from his chest in one long breath. That had been entirely too close.

The next instant, he spotted Andi.

She darted through the doorway and threw her arms around his neck. Her head pressed into his chest, the flowery scent of her shampoo filling his nostrils.

"I'm so glad you're okay," she murmured. "I thought for a minute . . ."

"I know," he whispered into her hair. "Me too. You did a good job, Andi. Thank you."

She pulled away from him and nodded.

Then she abruptly broke eye contact.

Probably so he couldn't see the emotion in her gaze.

But it was too late.

She had really been worried about him.

Knowing she cared so much about him made Duke's heart do flips.

He hated the situation that they were in. Hated that Celeste was between them. Hated that he still wanted closure with his fiancée—former fiancée. He still wasn't sure how to think of Celeste.

Now he would be cleaning up more messes Celeste had made—or that someone pretending to be her had made.

He had a feeling that this was just the beginning, but he dreaded learning what else might be in store.

twenty-four
Then

SHE FELT LIKE A NEW PERSON.

She couldn't explain why.

But over the past month or two, she'd had a new bounce in her step. Her thoughts had been more focused. Some of her anxiety had disappeared.

She continued with life as normal. Going to work. Going out with her friends. Doing all the things she always did.

Even her friends had noticed a new calmness about her.

She claimed it was because she'd been sleeping better lately. Maybe that was part of it. But the truth was she didn't fully understand why this was happening.

She wasn't complaining, even if she couldn't explain everything.

The only weird thing was that she sometimes had blank spaces in her mind.

Periods of time she couldn't recall.

Those blackouts bothered her.

Why couldn't she remember?

She didn't drink. Didn't take any medication to cause this.

Things had seemed normal for a while.

Then the other day, she'd left to grab a bite to eat.

Instead of heading to her favorite restaurant, she'd found herself at the mall.

Shopping.

Shopping? She'd never been much of a shopper.

Then she felt herself walking toward the food court.

Being drawn to a man sitting at a table there.

It wasn't like her, but she'd approached him and struck up a conversation. She hadn't even been nervous about it.

Really, it was all very strange.

She didn't know what was going on. Was this a test?

She'd thought about going to the doctor and getting a brain scan. Or maybe asking a friend who worked in the medical field what could cause this.

What if she had a brain tumor? Would that explain her personality changes? The blackouts?

It seemed like it might.

She sat across from the man. He was good-looking with a quick smile.

He shoved something across the table toward her.

A file.

"You'll want this," he murmured.

She only stared at it. "What is it?"

"Open it and you'll see."

She stole another glance at him before gingerly opening the folder.

Instructions were inside.

"We're moving forward," the man told her.

Somehow, she understood.

Then she reached into her purse. Pulled out a bottle with pills inside.

She handed it to him. "For you."

He grinned and took the bottle from her. Then he slipped it into his pocket.

"Very good," he told her. "You passed."

"I passed?" What was he talking about?

"You'll see," he murmured. "But we have big plans for you. Big plans."

A shudder rushed through her.

She didn't like the sound of that.

But she felt powerless to stop whatever was about to happen.

twenty-five
Now

ANDI AND DUKE had been directed to stick around the crime scene for the next few hours so police could question them.

Andi sat in the back of an SUV, the hatch open above her while Duke was with Gibson, O'Brian, and Ruby. They were close enough for her to hear the conversation.

"Did you actually see Kelly Hanson/Celeste Dawson taking care of your husband when he was in the hospital?" O'Brian asked.

"I did," Ruby said, her hands cuffed behind her. "She was beautiful. Hard to miss."

"Did you ever notice anything suspicious about her?"

"She truly seemed nice, like she cared. She mentioned once that she'd do whatever was within her power to help his pain." Ruby frowned. "It was terrible near the end, and we knew without a miracle Dustin wouldn't be around much longer."

"Was he in the hospital the whole time?"

"No. He came home for a while. Went to a special treatment facility to try some 'groundbreaking' infusions. Unfortunately, all of it was for nothing. The infusions didn't help."

"Which infusion center was this?" Duke squinted as he continued to gather information.

She shrugged. "I have no idea. They came and picked him up, took him for the treatments, and dropped him off several hours later. They said that because of the nature of the treatments, only patients and staff could be on the premises."

"So you didn't go there with him?" Gibson said.

"No, I didn't. It doesn't matter. The treatments didn't work." She paused. "Wait—do you think that's where he was drugged?"

"We're just collecting information," O'Brian said before leading her to a squad car.

As Andi watched her, exhaustion pressed on her.

Today had been a lot.

Fearing Duke might be killed had left her emotionally drained.

Now all the danger and uncertainty was taking a toll on her body and her mind, making her feel achy and fatigued.

The day wasn't even over yet.

She glanced at her watch.

In only two hours, Duke was supposed to meet with Celeste—or whoever had left that note.

Andi knew with certainty that O'Brian hadn't forgotten about it.

She wasn't sure exactly what to think of it. But her gut told her the meeting would only bring more trouble.

She wasn't surprised when, thirty minutes later, O'Brian made his way toward her, Duke at his side.

She waited for one of them to start.

O'Brian jumped in. "We're going to set up a sting at the location tonight. See if Kelly—Celeste—shows up."

"So you can arrest her." Andi stole a glance at Duke and saw the heaviness fill his gaze.

He let out a long breath as he turned to her. "I've been talking to them about it. I agreed that was okay, that it was the best choice."

Surprise washed through her.

That was a big step for Duke. He'd been so protective of Celeste. It must be killing him to set her up like this.

But if Celeste really had sent that note, she had to know Duke would do the right thing. That even though he might have considered keeping it quiet, that in the end he would probably tell the authorities. That this could be a trap.

Right?

Although Duke had told Andi on many occasions about the changes in his life since Celeste disappeared.

A friend had taken him to a Bible study, and Duke's entire life had been turned around. He found a reason to live other than for himself. He'd realized his own weaknesses and had discovered the power of grace and forgiveness.

She loved hearing him talk about it.

In fact, his transformation had softened Andi and made her more receptive to God as well. She'd been talking to Him more lately. Had been reminded that there was more to this life than just living and dying.

She looked up at Duke, realizing he was waiting for her reaction. "If that's what you think is best."

He nodded grimly. "I do."

"I'd love to be somewhere close."

"We figured you'd say that," O'Brian said. "Obviously, you can't be anywhere near where the two of them are meeting. But Gibson has volunteered to let you stay in his vehicle so you can keep an eye on things."

"I appreciate it."

"Great." O'Brian straightened and glanced at his watch. "We're leaving here soon so we can get things set up. Hold tight a few more minutes."

As he walked away, he left her and Duke alone a moment.

Andi's throat burned with words she wanted to say.

How she wanted to let him know she cared.

But she wasn't sure saying any of those things out loud would be a good idea.

DUKE STARED AT ANDI, wondering what was going through her head.

He wanted to ask. Yet he didn't.

She climbed from the back of the SUV where she'd been sitting and set the water bottle she'd been nursing on the bumper. Even though it wasn't that chilly outside, she had a blanket around her.

"That was close back there." Andi expertly changed the subject.

Duke nodded slowly before saying equally as slowly, "It was."

"You sure you're okay doing this tonight?" Her wide eyes implored his, and Duke could tell she was showing restraint with her questions.

He let out a long breath, not wanting to skirt around the truth. "I'm not sure about anything. But I think it's the right thing to do."

Approval swept through her eyes. "It is. If Celeste is innocent then maybe she can prove her case when she talks to the feds."

"Maybe." But Duke didn't sound convinced, even to his own ears.

Andi stole a glance at him from the corner of her eyes. "You really think Celeste is going to show up?"

He rubbed his jaw, pressure still stretching across his chest. "It's really hard to say. I'm not sure."

She paused, unspoken conversations hovering in her gaze. Finally, she asked, "What can I do for you?"

"I think you've already done more than enough. You've been there with me through thick and thin." His gaze locked with hers. "Thank you."

Yes, there were definitely unspoken conversations happening between them now.

Conversations about their past and their future. About how they cared about each other. But none of those topics seemed appropriate to discuss right now.

Even so, Duke wanted Andi to know how much he appreciated her.

He licked his lips, mentally rehearsing what he might say.

Before he could voice his thoughts aloud, Gibson strode toward them, interrupting any further conversation.

Maybe it was just as well, Duke mused.

Given the chance, he might just tell Andi exactly how much she meant to him.

And he wasn't sure how she would take the news.

twenty-six

DUKE PULLED his SUV onto the University of Fairbanks campus. He parked in the familiar spot and hesitated a moment in his car.

He knew he was doing the right thing. But sometimes doing the right thing could break your heart.

All he wanted was a moment to talk to Celeste alone. To hear her story. Maybe to understand.

But none of that would be happening.

As soon as the feds caught sight of her, Celeste would be arrested and brought in for questioning.

And possibly charged with the deaths of ten people.

No matter what kind of new information was uncovered, Duke still didn't believe she was capable of these murders. Unless Celeste looked him in the eye and confessed, nothing anyone said would change his mind.

He lifted a quick prayer before opening his SUV door.

Though he couldn't see the undercover FBI agents hovering nearby, he knew they were close. Sitting in cars. Pretending to jog. Looking like students making late night runs on the campus.

They were good at their jobs. He had no doubt they'd blend in.

But he also had no doubt Celeste would be skeptical. That she'd be coming into this with her eyes wide open. That at the first sign anything was amiss, she would flee.

He pulled on a sweatshirt since the air had become cooler as the sun disappeared.

Then he walked to the overlook.

On clear days, he could barely see Denali from this spot. Even when he could see it, the Great One, as many locals called it, was still far away.

But Celeste had delighted in each sighting they'd had together.

Out of the twenty or so times they'd been here, they'd only seen the mountain twice.

But those two times had been worth it.

Duke hadn't mentioned this to Andi because it felt too personal, but this had been where he proposed to Celeste. She'd come for a visit. He'd taken her out to eat, and then he'd brought her here.

The night had been perfect and clear.

Their future together had seemed so full of hope.

Celeste had moved here and gotten a job at the local

hospital. They'd been planning their wedding. She'd seemed happy.

Then everything had been turned upside down.

They'd only been engaged for three months when she disappeared.

The soles of his boots made soft thudding sounds as he paced the overlook.

He shoved his hands into the pockets of his jeans as he paused near a black railing and looked out.

Streetlights shone in the distance.

No mountains could be seen, not with the darkness and cloud cover. Yet Duke knew they were still there.

Just like he knew God was still there. Even when Duke couldn't see Him or feel Him, that didn't mean He had disappeared.

Duke tried to pull in a deep breath, but the action made him realize just how tight his lungs were.

He glanced at his watch.

It was 9:30. Celeste was supposed to be here anytime now.

Maybe tonight he'd finally get the answers he'd been waiting two years for.

He glanced around, looking for any signs of movement.

He spotted a man jogging past.

A car went by on a street below.

Both feds. Duke was nearly certain of it.

If Celeste was here, she was being cautious. She might

even be present right now but watching to see if this was a trap.

Which was why Duke couldn't show any indications he was working with the feds.

––––––

ANDI SQUIRMED in her seat as she waited in the SUV with the tinted windows.

Gibson's SUV.

To her surprise, they'd left her here unsupervised.

She'd been keeping her eye on the time. Celeste was fifteen minutes late.

Did that mean she wasn't going to show? Or was she simply being cautious?

A bad feeling lingered in Andi's gut. It was like when she disobeyed a superior and knew they'd found out and she'd have to face the music.

The one thing she wasn't usually great at was waiting and doing nothing.

Which was exactly what she was doing now.

She let out a sigh and glanced at the time again.

Celeste was now twenty minutes late.

Andi was getting antsy.

She could only imagine how Duke was feeling right now.

From where Andi sat in the parking lot, she had a view of the overlook. She saw Duke standing there, a stoic expression on his face. He also kept glancing at his watch.

She'd seen the same FBI agent jog by a couple of times. Had seen another agent drive past. Had seen another one dressed as a student strolling by with a backpack as if headed to a study group.

How many times could these people go past without someone getting suspicious?

As she scanned the area again, movement in the woods caught her eye.

She sat up straighter, curious about what it was. The breeze moving a branch?

An animal?

Could be. But she didn't think so.

She continued to watch, waiting to see that movement again. Waiting for confirmation of her assumption.

Then she saw it.

A woman.

Behind one of the trees.

Peering up at Duke.

A woman who looked a lot like Celeste.

Andi's muscles tightened like a knot being jerked from both ends.

She quickly texted Gibson, praying he got her message in time.

Then she watched as Celeste slunk behind the tree.

Nothing happened for several minutes, and Andi wondered what the woman was doing.

The next instant, the shadowy figure took off in a run in the opposite direction.

twenty-seven

DUKE WONDERED how long he should wait.

How long until he should simply give up.

Because he was getting restless.

A movement to his left caught his eye, and he glanced down.

There between the parking lot and the woods . . . a woman darted across the pavement.

Celeste?

He squinted.

No, that was . . . Andi.

Andi?

What in the world was she doing?

She sprinted across the parking lot and into the woods surrounding the area.

Two FBI agents followed her.

She'd seen something, hadn't she? She wasn't one to act irrationally.

Had she seen . . . Celeste?

He lunged from the lookout and headed down a small walkway.

Just as he reached the woods, he saw Andi dive to the ground.

Had she just tackled someone?

Lights shone on the ground, illuminating two figures.

Andi and . . . another blonde.

Was that Celeste?

His heart pounded harder.

He quickly closed the space between them, desperate to see with his own eyes who it was.

"Get off me," a woman cried.

Andi had the woman on her stomach, her arms held behind her.

O'Brian and several other agents surrounded them.

They pulled Andi off the woman.

Then the agents grabbed the woman's arms and jerked her to her feet.

The blonde's back still faced Duke.

He braced himself to see the woman who'd walked out of his life two years ago.

———

ANDI TOOK several deep gulps of air.

But she never took her eyes off Celeste as two agents grasped her arms.

This woman had caused so much heartache over the past couple of years that there was no way Andi would let her get away.

She didn't care if there was dirt on her knees and elbows. Leaves and twigs in her hair. That her shirt had become untucked.

All that mattered was catching this woman.

O'Brian instructed his agents to turn the woman toward them.

When Andi saw her face, her mouth dropped open.

This wasn't Celeste. It was a woman who looked very, very similar. From her blonde hair to her pert chin, to her aquiline nose—the two could be sisters.

"Who are you?" Duke's words came out as a growl.

The woman stared at them, fear in her eyes. "I don't know what's going on here. But you've made a mistake."

"Who are you?" O'Brian repeated Duke's question, appearing unamused by this turn of events.

"I'm Brianna Martin," the woman rushed. "I'm from Anchorage. I was hired to come up here for a job. I don't know what's going on or why you have your guns pointed at me."

O'Brian motioned for his guys to lower their weapons.

Then he turned back to her. "You're going to need to explain that some more."

Brianna shook her head, her eyes still darting about

frantically. "Look, I'm an actress. I was told I needed to come here and meet someone. That was it. It was a simple gig where I could make five hundred dollars—and I need the money. The person who hired me didn't say anything about *the feds* being here or being tackled by that woman."

She scowled at Andi as she dusted the dirt off her pants legs.

"Who hired you?" O'Brian asked.

"I don't know!" Brianna snapped. "We never met in person. This person left cash for me outside my house, and we only spoke over the phone."

O'Brian let out a heavy breath and then raked his hand through his hair as he turned away, almost as if he couldn't stomach what had just happened.

Andi's gaze went to Duke.

He looked equally frustrated as a shadow fell over his eyes and his jaw tightened.

For a moment, he'd really thought this woman was Celeste, hadn't he? So had Andi.

Was this the woman from the security video Doris let him see? Was Brianna the one who'd left that note outside Duke's back door?

Andi knew it was a good possibility.

This had all been a setup.

But why? To play games with Duke's heart?

Or had this been a distraction from something else bigger?

"There's something I was supposed to give you," Brianna said. "I got spooked and was going to forget about it. But since we're all here . . ." She pulled something from her pocket and thrust it toward Duke. "Take this."

Duke stared at the paper in her outstretched hand. Then, after a moment of hesitation, he took it and turned it over.

Andi leaned close to see what it was.

It was a photo, she realized.

As Duke shone a light on it, she recognized it was a snapshot, probably taken from a video in a gas station. The small black-and-white photo showed Celeste and the man they knew as William Ladak. They stood inside the station, buying something at the counter.

Andi's heart pounded harder.

The date stamp on the photo indicated it was from five days ago.

Was this real? Or was it another trick?

twenty-eight

DUKE WAS IN A MOOD.

He wanted to deny it, but he couldn't.

He'd been so sure that woman was Celeste. Then when she wasn't . . . when she was simply a paid actor . . . an impending weight—one that had been teetering inside him for entirely too long—had finally broken free and crushed his heart.

O'Brian had told him he was free to go. Duke walked back to his SUV, Andi beside him. They both climbed inside.

As Duke drove, Andi didn't say anything for several minutes. Probably because there was nothing to say.

Or because there was *everything* to say, but neither of them knew where to start.

Thankfully, Mariella called just then. Andi put her phone on speaker as she answered.

"Hey, guys," Mariella started. "Any updates? We've all been anxiously waiting."

Andi glanced at him before shrugging. "Unfortunately, it didn't pan out."

"I'm sorry to hear that." Mariella's voice dropped low with disappointment. "I know we were all hoping for closure, Duke most of all."

"What's going on with you?" Andi sounded perkier than she looked with her troubled gaze and downturned lips.

"A couple of things," she started. "First of all, remember Staci Lockard?"

"She was the sixth victim in California," Andi said. "The one who didn't appear to be sick, am I right?"

"Right," Mariella said. "We've been looking into her, but we haven't made much headway. There's literally almost nothing about her online. Weird, right?"

"In this day and age, kind of," Andi said.

"I also wanted to let you know that a woman contacted us via email regarding the podcast," Mariella continued. "Her name is Olivia Stuart, and she says she was a friend of Kelly Hanson's from back in California. She wants to talk."

Duke's heart skipped a beat. Olivia?

He vaguely remembered Celeste mentioning an old friend named Livy once. He hadn't known the woman's last name, and he'd tried to find it after Celeste had disappeared so he could talk to her. He'd been unsuccessful.

Could this woman be that friend?

"Talk how?" Duke asked, a new urgency to his voice. "When?"

"Video chat. Tonight at eleven. I didn't want to answer without talking to you."

"How do you know this woman is legit?" Andi ran a hand through her hair, a touch of hesitation to her actions and words.

"I had Matthew look into her," Mariella explained. "She seems like the real thing."

"We're headed to the lodge now." Duke turned on a nearby street. "Be there soon."

Andi ended the call and put her phone away.

More silence stretched.

He didn't know what to say, and Andi didn't push.

But when they pulled up to the Grayling several minutes later, neither of them made a move to get out. They still had a little time before they talked to Olivia.

"I'm sorry, Duke," Andi finally said as she turned toward him. "I know that was disappointing, to say the least."

"I really thought it was her for a minute." He felt stoic as he said the words. Disappointment had drained any emotion from him.

"That was the point."

He hardly heard her. "I just don't understand why someone would go through all this trouble to set something like that up. It doesn't make sense."

"I've been thinking about that also, and I'm not sure. Is this all being done as revenge on you? Does someone just want to mess with your mind?"

He shook his head, which had started to throb. "I wish I knew. I'm tired of living like this. I'm tired of the questions haunting me."

"Anyone in your shoes would feel that way."

Duke glanced at Andi, so grateful for her friendship and understanding. She'd been his sanity over the past several months. His days didn't seem complete unless the two of them talked.

There were very few people he'd ever been able to say that about.

He cleared his throat. "Back there when you were on the phone with Ruby, the situation you mentioned . . . it was Stockton, wasn't it?"

Andi didn't talk about him much, but Duke was curious. Stockton had been her colleague, but he'd been killed by Victor—only Andi couldn't prove it.

Andi lowered her gaze. "It was. As you know, we dated for a while. But we discovered we were better being linked as friends than we were being linked romantically."

"Why was that?"

She shrugged, her gaze showing she was deep in thought. "I can't put my finger on it necessarily. I guess the chemistry was missing or that 'it' factor, the one that makes two people work well together."

"I imagine it was still hard to lose him."

"It was." Her voice softened. "He was a good friend. Realizing he wouldn't be in my life anymore turned everything upside down. It started me down this path I'm now on."

The path where she'd lost her law license. Dedicated her life to bringing Victor down—even if it meant becoming an ice road trucker and driving up to the ends of the earth.

Duke had definitely never met anyone like her before.

"He was actually the last guy I dated." Andi glanced up at Duke, a new vulnerability in her gaze.

Something about those words made his throat squeeze.

The thought of her ever dating anyone else . . . it made his heart twist into a knot.

Their gazes caught.

Even with debris in her hair and smudges of dirt on her cheek, she was beautiful. Loyal. Tough. Smart.

The list could go on and on.

Andi Slade was definitely someone special. Unforgettable. A woman you didn't let walk away without a fight.

Right now, more than ever, Duke wanted to lean forward. To pull her into his arms. To show her how he felt.

He thought she wanted that also.

He could see it in her gaze. Feel it in the air crackling between them.

The chemistry was undeniable.

What would it be like to just give in? To press his lips to hers? To forget his loyalty to Celeste, a woman who might not really exist?

Their gazes caught, and Duke reached for her, stroked a hair out of her eyes. His hand lingered near her cheek, and he brushed the soft skin there.

In an instant, Andi snapped from the moment and pulled away.

Duke dropped his hand.

"We should go in," Andi rushed.

She opened the door and started to climb out.

Duke's heart fell at her outright rejection.

But she was right.

The two of them had come this far.

Why not see this situation with Celeste through, at least for a little longer? If he and Andi dated, he wanted the slate to be clean.

No regrets. No lines crossed.

He knew Andi wanted that also.

Duke climbed out and walked into the lodge.

There was only one thing that might get his desire to kiss Andi out of his mind—the fact he'd be able to talk to this Olivia woman.

Maybe she was legit and knew something.

He hoped that was the case.

———

ANDI SAT at the round table in the conference room and watched as Matthew hooked up a laptop at the front of the room.

Everyone around the table looked exhausted. It had been a long day. A few people were even drinking the coffee that Alfonzo had brought into the room.

Not her. It was too late for the caffeine, especially if she wanted to get any sleep tonight.

This supposed friend of Celeste's must be a night owl. But, on the other hand, Andi was glad to get this conversation over with. She'd rather know now what this woman had to say than wait until tomorrow.

Matthew fiddled with a few more things on the computer until finally, a few minutes later, a woman's face appeared on the screen—a brunette with hair that came to her chin, a long neck, and dark eyes.

She looked like the kind of person who might hang out with Celeste. Something about their appearance and energy matched—not that Andi had ever met either of the women. That was just her gut feeling.

Mariella took the lead on the conversation. "Thank you for getting in contact with us."

"Of course." Olivia offered a tentative smile.

They went around the table and introduced themselves.

But Andi had a question pressing on her. "Thank you for speaking with us. But I have to ask: why are you coming forward now?"

Olivia pushed a strand of hair behind her ear. "Because of the news coverage, of course. I didn't really put things together until I heard what the reporter said."

"And what did you hear?" Duke asked. "How did you and Celeste—or Kelly—know each other?"

"The woman I've seen on these news stories is *definitely* Kelly. I don't know if that's her real name or not, but that's the name she used when she worked with me at the hospital."

"Which hospital was that?" Andi asked the question in part as a test. One could never be too certain when it came to trusting people.

"Northwest Regional in Burbank."

Olivia could have gotten that information online, but at least the name had rolled off her tongue easily.

"How long did you know her?" Andi continued, trying not to go into interrogation mode.

"We worked together for four years. We actually roomed together for a year. Kelly was a great nurse. She really loved what she did, and she excelled in the field."

That fit what Andi knew about Celeste. But it didn't offer them any new insight, other than the fact that Celeste and Kelly truly might be the same person. However, Andi had suspected that for a while now.

The question was, was Kelly the woman's real name or did she have an alias before that?

"So you've heard about these accusations against her,"

Duke said. "Did you see anything suspicious in your time working together?"

"Not really." Olivia paused and frowned. "Well, that's not exactly true."

Andi leaned closer, wanting to watch Olivia's expression on the screen. "What do you mean?"

"I mean, for the first three years, she did great. But the last year, right before she abruptly quit and moved away without ever contacting me again, she acted a little off, like she had something on her mind."

"Did anything change that might have caused that?" Duke twirled one of Mariella's shiny pink pens between his fingers.

"The only thing that really changed was that Kelly had taken on some type of moonlighting job."

Now that *was* interesting, Andi mused. "What kind of moonlighting job?"

Olivia shrugged. "That's the thing. It's weird because she didn't say. She said she wasn't supposed to talk about it. But she seemed to become more and more withdrawn the longer she worked on this project."

"She never gave you any hints what this project might be?" Andi thought that sounded suspicious within itself.

"No, I really can't say she did," Olivia said. "I assumed maybe she was doing some type of in-home health care. As you can imagine, living in Burbank is expensive. Even though nurses make decent money, it's still hard to afford things out here. It wasn't unusual for my colleagues to get side jobs."

Duke shifted, his gaze laser-focused on the screen. "I know you said you don't have any real idea what she was doing. But was there anything she said or did that might help point us to some theories or ideas? The name of a coworker? A location? Anything?"

As they waited for her to answer, her gaze drifted off screen, and her eyes widened.

"Olivia, is everything okay?" Duke asked.

"I . . . I heard something." Her hand covered her heart as she stared in the distance. "I think . . . I think someone might be in my house."

twenty-nine

DUKE'S MUSCLES TIGHTENED. "Olivia, I'm going to call the police."

"Wait one minute." She stood and disappeared off-screen.

Duke glanced around the table, his gaze stopping on Andi.

She held up her phone. "I already have the number of the local police in Burbank on hand. I can call them as soon as I have the go-ahead."

They continued to wait. As they did, worst-case scenarios fluttered through Duke's mind.

Did someone know Olivia was talking to them? Had they shown up in order to silence her?

Part of Duke wanted to call the police right now. But he wasn't even sure the Burbank PD would go to her house to check on her with so little information to go on.

A moment later, she reappeared, a frazzled look in her gaze. "Sorry about that. It was actually my cat. She knocked something off the table. I guess I'm a little paranoid."

Duke released his breath. She wasn't the only one.

"I thought for sure someone was following me yesterday," Olivia continued. "But they turned before my street. I guess my imagination is working overtime."

He didn't like the sound of that.

"You need to tell the police that," Duke said. "Just in case."

"You really think so?" Olivia stared at him through the screen.

Duke nodded. "I don't want to frighten you, but I really do."

Her eyes widened another moment before she nodded. "Okay, I'll do that."

Relief swept through him. Whatever was going on, it was dangerous.

He didn't want another dead body.

Olivia cleared her throat and then continued. "Like I was saying earlier, Kelly started this moonlighting job. At first, she seemed really happy. But as time went on, she began not acting like herself. She started talking about how life wasn't fair sometimes."

Duke's stomach tightened. "Go on."

"I asked her if she felt like she was making a difference at this new job," Olivia said.

"Wait . . . that sounds like a weird question," Mariella commented.

"Maybe for some people, but that's what we always asked ourselves on the job." Olivia tucked a hair behind her ear. "There were some days when working in the hospital was tough. When patients were more than cranky—when they were downright nasty. When the workload felt like more than we could handle. When the administration acted like jerks. But we always had to remind ourselves why we did what we did."

"What did Kelly say?" Duke asked.

"She said she wasn't making enough of a difference and nursing wasn't the way she thought it would be. She said she wanted to quit, that it wasn't the job for her, but that she'd signed an iron-clad contract."

An iron-clad contract? Interesting for a nurse.

"Anything else?" Andi asked.

Olivia drew in a shaky breath. "The last thing she said to me was, *I think I've done something terrible.* When she wouldn't explain further, I asked her what I could do to help, and she said there was nothing anyone could say or do. Then she quit her job at the hospital, moved out, and I never saw her again."

The gang exchanged glances. That sounded bad. *Really* bad.

Andi cleared her throat and shifted. "Thank you for sharing. Have you already told the police this?"

"I did. The feds came and talked to anyone who used

to work with Kelly. I basically told them what I told you." Olivia glanced away and rubbed her lips together, almost as if she had another thought.

"What is it, Olivia?" Andi asked.

"This might be nothing . . ."

"We'd love to hear it, even if it's nothing," Duke said.

"I saw one of her paystubs once. She was rooting through her purse for something, and it fell out. I picked it up for her, but she snatched it back as if I wasn't supposed to see it. Anyway, the name on it was Compassion Mission."

Compassion Mission? Duke had never heard of them before.

It sounded almost like a nonprofit.

He grabbed his phone and typed in the name of the organization. He waited for any results to pop up.

"I didn't bring it up earlier in our conversation because I did some research on it myself and tried to find out more about the company," Olivia continued with a frown. "But I couldn't. It didn't seem to exist. It made me think that maybe I'd misread the paystub. I don't want to send you on a wild goose chase . . ."

It didn't seem to exist? Red flags went up in his mind.

"Thank you for sharing that." Andi exchanged a look with Duke. "Anything is helpful. We'll sort out whatever you tell us and do our own research."

"I figured as much." Olivia rubbed her hands on her jeans. "The fact I can't find any mention of this company online is very strange. I mean, everything leaves a digital footprint, right?"

"I can attest to that." Matthew raised a finger in the air.

At a pause in the conversation, Mariella glanced at Duke, a cautious look in her eyes.

Then she turned back to Olivia and asked, "I'm not sure where we're going with this. But would it be okay if we used any part of this conversation for our podcast?"

Mariella stole another glance at Duke.

He kept his expression stoic.

"Of course," Olivia said. "Whatever you need. Although, I would really like to say that I hope Kelly isn't painted in a bad light. I don't think she's guilty of anything."

Duke understood that, though his doubt over her innocence was beginning to crack.

He hated to admit it. Maybe he'd never even say it out loud. But the thought was there and beginning to solidify.

"Thank you so much for your time," Mariella said. "If it's okay, we may be in touch with you if we have more questions."

"Of course. I hope you find the truth." Olivia waved her hand in a goodbye, and a moment later the screen went blank.

Once the computer was closed, they all turned to each other.

"Well?" Mariella started, a hopeful look in her gaze. "What did you guys think?"

"Kelly told Olivia that she'd done something terrible," Ranger said. "It sounds like she was doing something wrong and then realized the error of her ways."

"But was she killing people to end their suffering?" Andi asked. "Then after she'd already taken their lives, did she realize what she'd done was wrong?"

"It's the only thing that makes sense." Simmy shrugged, regret in her gaze as she glanced at him. "I'm sorry, Duke."

His jaw tightened. Her words might be true.

However, he didn't want to talk about it anymore. He needed some time to think everything through.

Duke stood. "I don't know about you guys, but I'm ready to go to bed. I need to sleep on all of this so I can sort out my thoughts. Maybe we could talk about this more in the morning?"

"Of course," Mariella said, hesitancy still present in her voice.

She was worried they wouldn't see eye to eye, wasn't she? That they'd have another falling out. That this podcast team might split as quickly as they'd come together.

The truth was . . . that could be a real possibility.

———

ANDI KNEW there was no way she could go to bed. Not after everything they'd just heard.

Alfonso always let them stay at the Grayling Lodge even though they had places here in town. It somehow made it easier to get away from their everyday life and focus on the task at hand.

Andi and Duke used Ranger's SUV earlier. While the rest of the gang had ice cream, they picked up Duke's 4Runner and then grabbed small travel bags for the weekend stay.

Then they headed back to the hotel. Duke insisted on following her, just in case.

As she stepped out of Ranger's SUV into the lodge's parking lot, she paused a moment and glanced around.

Why did she feel as if someone were watching her?

She scanned the cars but saw no one. Weird.

She shook off the feeling before stepping back inside with Duke. They headed down the hallway toward their separate rooms.

Andi reached her room first and paused. "I know what you're going to do when you get back to your room."

Duke's gaze remained stony. "What's that?"

"You're going to look up Compassion Mission." She nodded at her room. "Why don't we look together?"

He hesitated just a minute before nodding. "Sure."

She stepped into the room, Duke behind her. She went to a small dinette in the corner and grabbed her laptop. Duke pulled his chair around beside her and watched the computer as Andi searched for Compassion Mission.

There were a few vague references, but nothing that directly tied in with what Celeste may have been involved with.

She searched several different sites before finally sighing and leaning back in her chair. "I don't know where else to look."

Duke tried to hide his disappointment and ran a hand over his face. "Do you think that name was just a cover for something else?"

"I don't know. I just keep thinking about assisted suicide. Would the name Compassion Mission fit that? Maybe."

He ran a hand over his face again. "That's what I thought also. I still just have a hard time seeing Celeste do this. Nothing makes sense to me right now."

"It's a lot to comprehend." Andi pulled her hands from the computer and turned toward him, her gaze softening. "I'm just not even sure really what's going on. Is Celeste trying to contact you? Why now? Or if this is all being set up by someone else, then *why* is it being set up by someone else? What's their motive?"

"I've thought about those questions a thousand times, and I still don't have any clues." His gaze looked listless as he stared at the wall. "There's nothing we've discovered yet that points to any answers."

"Tomorrow is a new day. Maybe we'll get the break we've been looking for then."

"Maybe." Duke's gaze met hers. "Thank you for being a good friend to me throughout all of this, Andi."

Her throat tightened. Was this his way of putting her in the strictly friend zone?

She'd felt the tension between them earlier. She'd seen in Duke's eyes that he wanted to kiss her.

The truth was, she'd wanted to kiss him also.

But she couldn't, not when they were so close to having some resolution in this. If they were going to be together, they could wait a little longer. They'd already come this far.

But emotions were tricky. Maybe the almost-kiss had been a spur-of-the-moment decision. Maybe Duke now regretted it.

She cleared her throat—and her thoughts—as she snapped back to the present. "Of course. Whatever you need."

She also knew the truth was that if Duke were to find Celeste and the two of them were to rekindle what they'd had, Andi wasn't sure she could be around them.

She wasn't sure her heart could take it.

Either way, everything just needed to be put on hold.

With so much going on, there was no room for feelings to distract them.

thirty

I SAT OUTSIDE of the lodge. I wasn't even sure why. I wasn't accomplishing anything out here.

I wanted, however, to know what they were doing. What they were saying.

What they knew.

I couldn't let them learn too much.

I needed to encourage them somehow to back off.

I had a few ideas to explore, some more dastardly than others.

I pulled my ballcap down. I didn't want anyone to recognize me.

Then I climbed out of the car.

No one else was around, which would work in my favor.

I walked casually, knowing better than to draw any

attention. Then I went to the car, pulled out a box cutter, and slit the tires.

By morning, these suckers would be flat.

This wouldn't dissuade everyone too entirely much. But it would cause them a headache, at least.

I had one other thing I had already done. A smile curled my lips as I thought about it.

I imagined the whole gang sitting inside the hotel right now. Talking. Drinking their water. Eating the refreshments set out by Alfonzo.

I had done my research. I knew how these meetings worked.

So I'd acted accordingly.

With any luck, what I'd done would start kicking in tonight.

It wasn't going to be pretty.

But it would be worth it.

All it had taken was putting a secret ingredient into the complimentary food they'd been offered.

A secret ingredient that none of them would be able to taste.

That was the brilliance of it.

I smiled at the thought of it. Perhaps I smiled a little too widely.

Part of me wished that I could stick around to watch it all play out.

But that would be too risky.

In fact, it was risky for me to even be out in this parking lot right now.

I didn't want anyone to see my face.

That was why I needed to be subtle. If they kept pushing and pushing, then I would have to up my game.

I was already anticipating having to do so.

But for now, this would work. It would slow them down, at the very least.

And I would simply sit back and watch everything happen.

thirty-one

DUKE AWOKE EARLY the next day—not that he'd really gotten any sleep—when Ranger sent him a text.

He'd called Ranger last night and asked for a favor. Maybe Ranger had found something.

Wasting no time, Duke got showered and dressed. Before it was even 7:00 a.m., Duke headed to the lobby to meet his friend. He hoped to hear an update.

Ranger was already downing a cup of coffee as he stood outside on the deck looking at the river.

"Morning," Duke started as he joined him near the railing.

"Morning." Ranger crushed his empty cup and then tossed it into a metal trash can behind them. "I did what you asked."

"And?"

"I saw that guy again," Ranger said. "The one Andi thought was eavesdropping on us and ran away."

Duke's breath caught. "So he was outside the lodge?"

Ranger nodded. "He was. But I didn't approach him, and I don't think he saw me."

"What happened?" Duke's thoughts raced as he tried to anticipate what his friend might say.

"He stayed in the parking lot until about 1:30. Then he left and went back to a smaller motel here in town. I watched him go to his room. I stayed outside for a while to see if he would do anything else, but it appeared he'd turned in for the night."

Duke stored all that information away. "Anything else?"

"I got his license plate number. The car is a rental, of course. But I pulled a few strings, and I found out his name."

Duke didn't even bother to ask how Ranger had done it. It didn't matter.

"He's Kyle Bartiromo from Santa Monica, California."

"What else?"

"He works for some type of tech startup. Doesn't have any type of criminal history. In fact, the guy graduated at the top of his class from an elite private school and went to one of the top universities for engineering, where he also graduated at the top of his class."

Duke grunted. He'd expected someone with more

nefarious intentions or a more ambiguous background, he supposed.

"My first instinct was that this guy was a reporter or something," Ranger said. "But that doesn't appear to be the case."

"No, it doesn't." Duke pressed his lips together in thought. "So why does a guy from California with a background in technology want to eavesdrop on our conversations?"

Ranger's gaze caught his, and he tipped his head to the side. "That's an excellent question."

Duke let out a sigh and crossed his arms before turning back toward the river. "Did you find out what kind of tech firm this guy is working at?"

"I'm trying to find out more info. It's just called Restoration Tech. There's not much about it online. I'm going to keep looking."

"I appreciate you doing this," Duke told him. "I know you're tired and that you've had a lot going on."

Ranger shrugged as if it weren't a big deal. "I've been trained to survive on very little sleep. I'm going to be just fine."

Duke clamped his hand on his friend's arm. "You're a good man, Ranger Garrett. Thanks again for everything."

"One more thing. Simmy is sick."

Duke paused. "What do you mean?"

"Maybe she has a stomach bug or got food poisoning yesterday. She got sick last night and called me. Said she was okay for now. I'm keeping tabs on her this morning."

"I hope she feels better."

"Me too."

Now Duke needed to figure out exactly what he would do with the information Ranger had offered.

———

ANDI STOOD at the drink counter of the lodge and fixed herself some coffee—using a piece of the caramel candy she always carried with her and some half-and-half.

In college, her friends had called her the convenience store barista because she could make pretty amazing coffee shop style drinks using things she found in gas stations.

She'd never been able to justify spending so much money on expensive coffee drinks, not even when she started bringing in better cash flow as an attorney. Her chintzy drinks had become a part of her.

She took a sip of her makeshift caramel latte and stole another glance through the windows at the deck outside.

Whatever Duke and Ranger were talking about, the discussion looked intense. More than anything, Andi wanted to go out there. To hear their conversation. To be in the loop.

But Duke would share whatever he'd learned from Ranger with her in his own time. She hadn't been invited into that conversation, and she wanted to stay in her lane.

A few minutes later, the two men stepped back inside.

Andi tried to look casual as she called, "Good morning."

"Morning," Duke's gaze brightened when he saw her.

The fact didn't go unnoticed—and it brought Andi a small burst of pleasure.

The men joined her and grabbed fresh cups of coffee. She took a sip of her own, her thoughts still racing. Neither offered any insight to their conversation.

"It's about time to start our meeting, isn't it?" Duke raised his cup to his lips and took a sip.

Right on cue, Matthew appeared in the lobby. "Mariella won't be making it this morning. She's not feeling well."

"Neither is Simmy," Ranger said.

"Stomach bug or food poisoning?" Matthew asked.

Ranger nodded.

Talk about awful timing, Andi mused.

"Mariella wanted me to tell you that Alfonso said he brought in some pastries from a bakery for us," Matthew said. "They're in the conference room."

Andi wasn't especially hungry right now. She had too much on her mind.

Mostly Celeste, of course.

But she still hadn't forgotten about those men in the black van with duffel bags and tubs full of cash, electronics, guns, and pictures.

Those guys were connected to Victor, and she wanted

to figure out how. She wanted to figure out what they were up to.

First and foremost, they needed to figure out the Celeste situation.

They all headed to the conference room, ready to get started on their day.

thirty-two

MARIELLA JOINED them via video call and said she was feeling a little better. She and Simmy had both had some ice cream last night, so maybe it was food poisoning instead of the stomach bug. Ranger and Matthew had passed on the late-night dessert.

Mariella didn't mention anything about finances or social media ratings or Alpine.

She focused on Celeste.

For that, Duke was grateful.

As the meeting wrapped up, Mariella added that Alpine was supposed to make a big announcement later today. She wasn't sure what it might be, but she wanted everyone to be aware. They were, after all, associated with the man now—for better or worse.

Then assignments went out. Matthew would continue to work behind the scenes while Ranger headed to the hotel and kept an eye on Kyle. Yes, Duke had told everyone about the man and the fact that Ranger had followed him last night.

There was no need to keep that a secret.

Duke and Andi, in the meantime, would follow up about Brianna as well as Olivia.

They left everyone to do their jobs, and Duke and Andi stepped into the lobby.

"Let me call Gibson," he started.

But, before he could, his phone rang.

A number appeared on his screen that he hadn't seen in years. Lane Sullivan, who also went by Sully. The two had worked together in the Army CID for a few years.

Duke excused himself to answer. "Hey, man. How's it going?"

"Pretty good," Sully said. "I wish I was calling just to catch up."

"I figured as much. What's going on?"

"Can you swing by the office later today? There's something I want to talk to you about—alone. CID matters, you know?"

Duke glanced at Andi. "I can do that. Name the time."

"Four o'clock work?"

"I'll be there."

He ended the call and explained to Andi that it was a former colleague. Then, before he got distracted, he dialed Gibson.

He knew there was a good chance the state trooper wouldn't give him any updates, but it was worth a try.

Gibson answered on the first ring. "I was just thinking about you guys."

Duke raised his eyebrows at Andi. "Any chance you can give us an update?"

"As a matter of fact, there *is* an update I can give you. First of all, it appears Brianna's story is true. She was paid five hundred dollars by a woman whom she never met in person to show up last night and deliver that picture."

"Does she know who the woman was?"

"Unfortunately, no. Their interactions were online. We're trying to track down this woman now, but it's going to be an uphill battle."

"I can imagine," Duke said. "Anything else?"

"We were able to track down the location where that photo of Kelly/Celeste and William Ladak was taken," Gibson said. "The photo Brianna had."

Duke sucked in a breath as he anticipated what Gibson might say. "And?"

"It was taken at a place called Gus's Gas, a station about forty miles outside Fairbanks toward Tok. The date stamped on it is accurate. It appears to have been taken five days ago."

"Did they run any type of facial recognition that might show if it really is Celeste?" Andi asked, stepping close enough to the phone that Duke caught a whiff of her vanilla-scented shampoo.

Duke resisted the urge to inhale for any longer than necessary and reminded himself to stay focused.

"It's hard to say for sure, but it definitely looks like Celeste and William," Gibson said.

Duke's throat tightened. "I assume you guys have been out there to talk to the people at the gas station?"

"The feds went this morning. I'm only their liaison with the state police. Anyway, they didn't come back with much new information. But I figured I owed it to you to tell you that much."

They thanked Gibson and ended the call.

Then Andi glanced up at Duke. "Why do I have a feeling we're taking a trip out to Gus's Gas?"

"It's like you read my mind."

Andi nodded outside. "Then let's go."

ANDI AND DUKE pulled up to Gus's Gas forty minutes later.

Once she saw the small, beige building with streaks of black tar coming from the flat roof, she instantly tried to picture Celeste coming in here. Or Kelly. Andi wasn't really sure how to refer to the woman anymore.

Why would she stay so close? It still didn't make any sense, no matter what angle Andi tried to come at it from. If Celeste wanted to run and hide, she should have left

Alaska, not remained in Fairbanks or anywhere relatively close.

Maybe she and Duke would find some answers inside the station.

A man with scruffy white hair and an oversized mustache that covered his upper lip worked behind the counter. He glanced up, looking rather bored as Duke and Andi walked in.

"Good morning," he muttered.

"Morning." Duke strode to the counter and paused. "I was hoping you could help me with something."

The man's lips curled down in a frown. "You here asking about the picture of that woman and man?"

Duke tilted his head. "How did you know?"

"Just got that sense about you when you walked in." The man paused and glanced back and forth between them. "You feds? Because you two don't strike me as feds."

"Actually, the woman in that picture is my . . ." Duke swallowed hard before finally saying, "fiancée."

Andi noticed he used the present tense. Not *was* my fiancée or my *ex*-fiancée.

But my *fiancée*.

She tried to swallow the lump in her throat.

She'd never heard him refer to Celeste like that before. Or maybe she had at first, but not recently. For some reason, it bugged her.

The clerk's eyebrows shot up. "Fiancée? That's a twist I didn't see coming."

"I've been searching for her for the past two years, and I'm trying to make sure she's okay. Were you here the night she and that man came in?"

The man smoothed his mustache with his thumb and index finger before nodding. "I was. But I'm afraid the rest of what I have to say will disappoint you. I don't really remember much about them. They came in and got gas. He bought a bottle of water, and she got some orange juice, I think. Pretty sure they got a bag of chips to split. That was it."

"How did they act?" Duke asked.

He shrugged. "Normal. Nothing suspicious. That's probably why I didn't really pay much attention to them. They seemed ordinary."

"Was that the first time you'd seen them in here?" Andi didn't want to miss any details that could later be important.

"As a matter of fact, it wasn't." He smoothed his mustache again. "I saw them one other time."

Duke perked with interest at his words. "When was that?"

"Oh, I don't know . . ." The clerked sighed before shrugging. "Probably about a month ago."

Andi's thoughts raced.

This man remembered seeing Kelly/Celeste and William/Bobby in here twice. But that didn't mean they hadn't been here other times as well, times this clerk couldn't recall or when someone else might have been working.

Did that mean that when Kelly/Celeste and William/Bobby had fled Fairbanks that they'd headed this way?

It seemed like a possibility.

"Do you by chance remember what kind of vehicle they were driving?" Duke asked.

"The feds had me look that up this morning also. I couldn't make out a license plate number, but the vehicle was a dark green Ford Bronco."

Before they could talk more, the door opened and another customer came inside.

Andi knew this conversation was over.

But maybe this trip hadn't been for nothing.

They were slowly inching closer to the truth.

Maybe she didn't have any answers about Victor yet. But Duke finding some closure with Celeste would be the next best thing.

thirty-three

"THERE'S one thing I know for sure," Duke said as he and Andi headed away from the gas station. "If there's any state a person should go to in order to disappear, it's Alaska. There are miles upon miles of land that are uninhabited. It makes it almost impossible to find somebody who really wants to hide."

Andi nodded and popped a cheese curl into her mouth. She'd decided to buy a snack before they left.

"So you're thinking that even if Celeste is staying somewhere in this general vicinity that locating her would be nearly impossible, am I right?" Andi said.

He nodded, his earlier grimness beginning to settle in again. "Unfortunately, yes. Granted, the FBI has more resources than I do. They might be able to send a drone up or look at satellite footage. But searching this amount of land . . . it would take years."

"But at least it's something." Andi munched on another cheese curl.

He nodded slowly. "It is something."

Twenty miles out from Fairbanks, Duke's phone buzzed. He glanced at the number on the screen and, without missing a beat, he pulled off onto the shoulder, braking hard.

This couldn't wait.

"Have you lost your mind?" Andi's voice rose as she reached for the grab bar above her. "What are you doing?"

"I asked Matthew to search the dark web for anything he could find on Compassion Mission. Basically, what we believe to be true is that there's nothing on the internet about Compassion Mission. So, in order to find out anything we have to go deeper into the dark web to places normal people don't have access to."

"And?" Andi stared at his phone.

Duke grabbed it and clicked on the message that Matthew had sent.

I found a mention of Compassion Mission on the dark web. It was on a server where people with terminal diagnoses were basically being "brokered" with various options that could help them live longer. One message in particular mentioned a man named Paul Brantley. It was sent two and a half years ago, and I thought you might be interested.

As soon as the message popped up, Duke clicked on it.

I've heard about what you're doing, and I'd love to consult with you about some options. I can meet at two p.m. in the atrium at the library. I look forward to hearing more.

Duke looked at the date. Two and a half years ago, just like Matthew had said.

He quickly Googled the man. He was fifty-seven and worked in finance.

And . . .

Duke's eyes widened. He resided in Fairbanks.

Two and a half years ago Celeste had worked in Fairbanks. That was when she'd been accused of killing those people at Tanana Regional.

Had Celeste been the one meeting with Paul? Had she continued her work with Compassion Mission even after moving to Fairbanks?

Duke had to talk to this Paul guy.

He turned to Andi. "We need to see if we can find Paul Brantley."

"I'm already on it." Andi typed something on her phone. A few seconds later, she said, "I have an address. What do you say we go give this guy a visit?"

"Just tell me where."

———

TWENTY MINUTES LATER, Andi and Duke pulled in front of a small house in a small neighborhood with oversized lots. A ramp led from the driveway, over the porch steps and to the front door.

On the way there, they'd researched more about this Paul guy.

From what Andi had gathered, the man was in a car accident four years ago that had rendered him a paraplegic. He wasn't married, nor did he have any kids.

Andi's gut told her this meeting was important. That she and Duke would learn something significant.

She hoped that gut feeling was correct.

Duke charged forward, heading up the ramp and toward the door as if on a mission—because he was. Andi scrambled to keep up.

Just as she paused beside him, he knocked.

Noises sounded from inside. A moment later, the door opened.

A thin man with balding hair and glasses appeared. He wore a light-blue polo shirt and black slacks.

He was in a manual wheelchair. "Can I help you?"

"We're looking for Paul Brantley," Duke started.

The man's gaze clouded with suspicion. "That's me. What do you want? If you're selling something, I'm not interested."

"We're not selling anything," Duke rushed. "And I apologize for stopping by uninvited. I'm Duke McAllister, and this is my colleague, Andi Slade. We're looking into an organization called Compassion Mission, and we were hoping you could answer some questions."

The man's face turned pale, and he rolled back, starting to shut the door. "I don't have anything to say."

"Please . . ." Duke stepped closer. "It's important."

But it was too late. The man slammed the door.

Duke pounded on the door again. "I need some answers. Kelly Hanson aka Celeste Dawson was my fiancée. I'm trying to figure out what happened to her. I believe you may have some answers for us."

Silence stretched on the other side of the door.

"Please," Duke continued. "We keep hitting dead ends. I think you know something that could help us find her and bring closure for people who have lost loved ones."

More silence.

After a few more minutes, Duke muttered something underneath his breath. Then he turned, his jaw hardening and his gaze tumultuous.

From what Andi had heard, the old Duke would have probably slammed his fist into the side of the wall or busted the door down.

But the new Duke practiced self-control. He turned to prayer instead of emotional reactions.

However, Andi could tell he was struggling now.

"He won't talk." Andi kept her words gentle.

Duke rubbed his jaw. When his gaze met hers, Andi knew he was on the verge of doing something he might regret. On the verge of demanding answers or letting Paul know just how urgent this situation was.

"This guy is our only lead," Duke finally said. "If he doesn't talk, then I don't know how we're going to find Celeste."

Andi couldn't argue with that statement.

Duke turned toward the door again and pounded on it one last time. "Please. Talk to us."

Just as before, silence stretched on the other side.

The man was clearly spooked. Whatever Compassion Mission was, even the name of it frightened him.

Was that because he knew something about these supposed mercy killings?

It would only be a matter of time before the FBI tracked this guy down also. But it seemed a shame to walk away without any leads.

However, their hands were tied. They couldn't force the man to talk—not legally and ethically, at least.

Duke pulled out a business card and stuck it in the door.

Maybe—just maybe—the man would have a change of heart and call.

Andi hoped that would be the case.

thirty-four

DUKE TRIED to keep his anger at bay as he headed down the road.

He desperately needed Paul to talk to him. But he couldn't force the man to do so. Trying to do that would only get Duke arrested, and that was the last thing he needed right now.

Thankfully, at just that moment, Ranger called.

"What's up?" Duke started.

"Kyle is on the move."

Duke straightened. "Where are you?"

"On the southwest side of town near the airport," Ranger said. "I've been following him."

"Keep an eye on him. I'm headed that way. Please keep me updated on where you're going."

"Got it." Ranger paused. "One other thing. I thought

you should know that Mariella's tires were slashed last night."

"What?" Andi glanced at Duke, her eyes narrowed.

"I discovered it this morning. It must have happened before I started to keep watch. I didn't think to check everyone's vehicles. Anyway, I looked at Mariella's car myself, but I didn't find anything that might tell us who's responsible. I even asked Alfonso to check security footage of the parking lot. A dark figure came out of nowhere and slashed the tires before disappearing into the darkness. I tried to search the other security feeds, but I didn't find anything."

"Could you tell if it was a man or woman?" Duke asked.

"Unfortunately, no. It was too dark."

"I'm sorry to hear that," Duke muttered.

The team was clearly starting to make someone nervous.

Nervous criminals did stupid things.

Duke headed toward the airport. He hoped Kyle wasn't trying to leave the area. If so, they'd need to stall him before he caught a flight.

Duke needed to know why this guy was watching them. What his connection was. What the man knew.

Ranger spouted out directions as he tailed the man.

A few minutes later, Duke pulled into Darling Dolly's, a local homestyle restaurant and dive.

Perfect, Duke mused. Kyle hadn't gone to the airport.

Hopefully, they could corner this guy and find out some information.

Duke pulled into the lot and put his SUV in Park.

Then he waited to see if anyone else went inside to meet Kyle.

———

"WHAT'S your play going to be?" Andi asked.

She stared at the restaurant, a small, one-story structure with a bright coral thatched roof. All the signage was hand-painted and chintzy, but based on the number of cars in the lot, this was a local favorite.

Duke had signaled to Ranger that he could leave.

Andi hoped that wasn't a bad call, that this guy wasn't dangerous, and they wouldn't need backup.

"I want to make sure no one is going in there to meet with him first." Duke scanned the parking lot. "Because if he's meeting someone, then learning who that person is could also be valuable."

She crossed her arms and settled back in her seat. "Good thinking. How long do we wait?"

His jaw twitched. "Ten minutes. Then we go inside and have a heart-to-heart with this guy."

Andi let out a breath as she tried to think everything through. "I still can't figure out for the life of me who this guy is. Maybe he's a reporter."

"I don't know. I only know he's a little too curious about our podcast. That makes me uncomfortable."

Andi stole a glance at him. "I know it probably doesn't feel like this, but we're inching closer and closer to finding answers."

His gaze clouded. "I hope so. Because this whole thing has left me puzzled for entirely too long."

"I understand. I do wish Paul had talked to us. The fact that he's paraplegic . . ."

"I know. Believe me, I know."

Ten minutes passed, and no one else went inside the restaurant. Maybe this guy wasn't meeting someone after all.

Finally, Duke and Andi climbed from the SUV and stepped into Dolly's. The inside matched the exterior. Outdated tables, wood-paneled walls. Ruffled curtains.

It smelled like mama's homemade cooking, and "Nine to Five" played overhead.

Duke went straight for Kyle's table.

As they approached, Kyle looked up, and his eyes widened behind his trendy glasses. The scrawny man scrambled back in the booth as if frightened.

Duke slid in beside him and Andi across from him.

"We'd like to have a little conversation with you," Duke said.

"Is . . . is that right?" Kyle stammered the words out, clearly nervous.

"You've been following us," Duke continued.

"I—I . . . I have."

At least he didn't deny it, Andi mused.

"Why?" Duke demanded. "And don't make excuses. I'm willing to stay here as long as necessary until I get some answers."

"It's not what you think." The man's words collided with each other in his rush to get them out.

"Then please explain." Duke's gaze locked on him, practically pinning him in place.

"I've actually been trying to build up the nerve to speak with you." His voice trembled. "I . . . I just haven't brought myself to do it yet."

Interesting explanation, Andi thought before asking, "What did you want to speak with us about?"

"Compassion Mission."

thirty-five

DUKE'S BREATH caught at the mention of the organization Olivia had also brought up—an organization that seemed to be like a ghost.

"What do you know about Compassion Mission?" Duke asked.

"I work for them." Kyle shrugged as if that should have been a foregone conclusion.

"I thought you worked for Technology Revolution."

"I do. It's . . . it's just an arm of Compassion Mission. Same company, though."

"And why did you want to talk to us?" Duke continued to push.

The waitress appeared and asked them if they wanted drinks.

Duke's stark *no* must have been a little too emphatic. The woman raised her eyebrows and stepped back.

The good news was she probably wouldn't be back to interrupt them again.

"I don't like some of the things I've seen going on." Kyle lowered his voice here. "I needed to tell someone. I've listened to your podcast, and I know what you guys are doing. So I came here to tell you. But . . ."

"But what?" Andi asked.

He tugged his collar again. "The stakes are high, to say the least. If my boss finds out I'm here talking to you . . . then I'm as good as gone."

Duke didn't like the sound of that. "We appreciate the risk you're taking. What has you so flustered?"

Kyle ran a hand through his dirty-blond hair. "I started working for Compassion Mission about five years ago. It sounded like a really good organization. But as I got deeper into it, I could see that things weren't quite right."

"What do you mean?" Andi stared at Kyle, all her focus on the conversation.

"I mean, we help people with life-altering disabilities and diagnoses to have better lives," Kyle said. "I head up the tech wing, so I try to develop things to accommodate people—shelves that are easier to reach, compliant bathrooms, things like that. I wanted to keep things on the cutting edge."

"Keep going." Andi crossed her arms as she settled in to listen.

"I worked with Kelly for a while. She had a big heart." Kyle paused. "There were some patients . . . well, there were some who just couldn't be helped. Their quality of life wasn't there, and there was no hope it would ever be there, no matter how we tried to make things easier. She wanted to help those whom nothing else had helped, and the only way to give those people relief was through death. I know it sounds terrible, but if you saw how some people suffered . . ."

"What did she do?" Duke's voice sounded hard, as if he didn't want to release any of his emotions or reactions. He only wanted to listen.

"She came up with a plan for how to end their lives without anyone ever knowing that was what had happened." Kyle took a long sip from his cup of water before continuing. "She said there was too much stigma if people knew, so it was better to do it in secret. The patients all agreed. None of them acted against their will. In fact, some of the patients begged her to help them. How could she say no?"

"I'm guessing things didn't go as smoothly as she hoped," Andi murmured.

Kyle rubbed his throat, his face ashen. "Our boss found out what was going on, and he was furious. He fired her."

"You mean, once he found out that Kelly had been killing patients?" Andi clarified.

"Yes, exactly." Kyle frowned. "Here's where things got even hairier. Instead of going to the police, he tried to cover it up. He said we were doing too much good to have his program shut down. Said it was better if we made the deaths look natural, then we could continue on with our work."

"How many people knew what was going on?" Duke asked.

"Only my boss, Michael Craig, and Kelly."

"But *you* knew . . ." Andi pointed out.

He took another long sip of water. "Not at first, I didn't. But I overheard a few things. When I talked to Michael about it, he convinced me to stay quiet for the sake of the company. He said so much would be lost. I thought I understood where he was coming from. I thought I could be silent. But I can't. Not anymore. At the same time, I don't know what to do."

Andi leaned closer. "Why come to Fairbanks and find us?"

"I've been trying to build up the courage to talk to you about it. But I know if I speak of this aloud, that things could go south fast." He swallowed hard. "I need someone who can help me make things right . . . before I'm killed."

———

ANDI LISTENED to what Kyle told them, tapping into her analytical side as she waded through his statements to find the truth.

"So instead of going to the police down in California

or the FBI even, you decided to fly up to Alaska and find us?" she clarified.

"I know it might sound crazy," he said. "But I did my research and thought you guys could help. Besides, I wanted to get as far away from Michael as I could. After all of that happened, he kind of lost his mind. He was doing some major damage control and . . . something about him changed. I think he's desperate."

"And that's why you're afraid you could be killed?" Andi asked.

Kyle nodded.

"Do you think you're safe here?" Duke asked.

Kyle sighed again. "I don't know. I really don't. Part of me feels as if I'm being watched. Then I think maybe that's crazy. I just don't really know."

"Are you willing to talk to the FBI about this?" Andi asked. "Because they're in town investigating right now. I'm sure this would be helpful."

He tugged at the collar of his shirt. Jerked his shoulders as if trying to work out some kinks. Rolled his neck.

They waited.

Finally, he said, "Honestly, I just don't know. I don't want my name and face out there."

On one hand, Andi could understand. On the other, if what Kyle had told them was true, he could be a valuable asset in bringing justice to this situation. The FBI could protect him in return for his testimony.

"How long are you going to be in town?" Duke asked.

"I don't know that either. I don't have much of a plan. I only know I needed to get away and tell somebody."

Andi glanced around the hometown restaurant. "Why come here? We thought that maybe you were meeting someone."

He shrugged. "I needed somewhere to eat, and I read reviews online saying this place was good. That's it."

To Andi, it seemed like someone in hiding might want to lie low. Order food in. Buy groceries and hang out in their hotel room.

But she supposed everyone acted differently under stress.

She reminded herself not to jump to any conclusions.

They needed to look into the people Kyle had mentioned. Verify some facts. Probably talk to Gibson or O'Brian.

Then maybe she and Duke could start to put together their case.

Maybe this nervous man sitting across from her in the booth was the missing link they'd needed all this time.

thirty-six

BACK IN THE CAR, Duke glanced at his watch.

He'd nearly forgotten about his meeting with Sully. He had just enough time to get to the Army CID office.

"I hate to do this to you, but that colleague who called me earlier . . . he needs to talk to me." He turned toward Andi and paused. "He asked to speak with me alone."

An unreadable emotion passed through her gaze before she nodded. "I understand. There are confidential matters from your old job. But he didn't say what it was about?"

Duke shrugged. "It's CID stuff, but he didn't want to talk about it over the phone. He made it sound like it couldn't wait. If it's okay, I'll drop you off at the lodge. That way, you'll have a vehicle if you need it. Then I'm going to head out to meet with him."

"That sounds like a plan." She clicked her seatbelt in

place as Duke pulled from the parking lot. "What do you think of this Kyle guy?"

Duke headed down the road, his thoughts drifting back to that conversation. "I'm not sure. It's a lot to process. It sounds like we need to look into the boss at the company. I'll be surprised if the FBI hasn't already done that."

"From the sounds of it, this guy may have denied what happened."

"True." Duke nodded. "Let's ask Matthew to look into him."

"I'll give the team the update when I get to the lodge. Maybe they'll have some thoughts on it also."

They pulled up at the Grayling, and he put his SUV in Park.

Andi paused as she reached for the door handle, and her gaze met his. "Be careful, and I hope your meeting goes well."

Duke appreciated the concern in her voice. At this point, nothing was to be taken lightly, not when there was so much on the line.

"You be careful too," he told her. "I don't know how long this will take, but let me call you . . . just in case the conversation is important."

————

ANDI WISHED she could go with Duke. Wished she could hear what his colleague had to say. But she truly did understand the boundaries in place right now. As a lawyer, she knew some discussions were on a need-to-know basis.

She headed into the Grayling Lodge and went straight to the conference room to meet the rest of the team.

Matthew sat at a table in the corner with his computer. Mariella, who was feeling better, recorded something for the podcast at another table. She released smaller weekly episodes to keep the listenership up in between their bigger podcasts.

Ranger and Simmy sat at the round table looking at some files. Simmy sipped what appeared to be some Sprite. She looked a little pale but otherwise okay.

As soon as Andi walked in, everyone glanced up at her. Instead of repeating herself more than once, she got everyone's attention and filled the team in on what Kyle had told them.

About how Kyle headed up the tech wing at Compassion Mission. About how Kelly/Celeste had worked there. About how some patients couldn't be helped and had a terrible quality of life. How Kelly/Celeste thought their only relief could be found in death. About how his boss, Michael Craig, found out and tried to cover it up.

Ranger leaned back in his chair as he listened, but his gaze was razor-sharp. "Is this guy willing to talk to the feds?"

"He's scared." Andi tapped her fingers on the table as she sorted through her thoughts. "He fears he'll be killed."

"I hate to say it, but this only makes Celeste look even more guilty." Simmy frowned as she said the words.

Andi nodded, unable to deny the truth.

Then she glanced at Ranger. "Enough about what Duke and I were up to. How about you?"

Ranger held up one of the photos he'd been studying. "We've been trying to examine each of the victims from the hospital here in Fairbanks. We figured it couldn't hurt to dig into their backgrounds a little more."

"Did you find out anything interesting?" she asked.

"Just one thing." Ranger held up a photo of a man. "This is Ricky Miller, the third victim. Turns out, he was friends with Craig Rogers."

Andi sucked in a breath and glanced at Simmy. Simmy was Craig's daughter, though she hadn't discovered that until after the man's death. He was the podcaster whose death had basically led their team to form.

"That's interesting . . ." Andi murmured.

"I thought so too," Ranger said.

Andi peered over his shoulder at the rest of the photos there, at all the lives that had been cut short. The first person she picked out in the lineup was Dustin Logan, Ruby's husband.

Then her gaze stopped at another photo. She squinted as she stared at it.

"What is it?" Simmy glanced at Andi then back at the photo.

Without saying anything, Andi picked up the picture and studied it another minute.

Her breaths came faster as she realized the face was familiar.

"Andi?" Ranger asked.

"Who is this?" She turned the photo toward them.

"That's James Parsons, the hospital administrator. Why?"

"I've seen him before." Andi rubbed her lips together after she said the words.

"You mean when you were at the hospital or something?" Simmy clarified.

"No, I saw his photo." She held it up. "I'm nearly certain this man's image was one of the pictures I saw in the back of the van I climbed into with those thugs."

thirty-seven

I WAS GOING to have to get more creative.

Clearly, the little present I'd left in their snacks wasn't enough. Nor were the slashed tires.

I didn't want to have to take more drastic measures.

But I would.

The good news was I was keeping an eye on them. I knew what they knew. I knew what they were planning—for the most part.

I could hear what they were saying in their little meetings—but only when they were in the conference room.

But they seemed to be doing a lot of their talking when they were away.

I knew about the men watching Andi.

Part of me hoped they'd take care of this group before I had to do it.

I didn't want to deal with these people.

But they had left me no choice.

This was all their fault.

They were too good at what they did.

I had read up on their case history. I knew about their success rates.

When these six people got together, they could do amazing things. They each had different skill sets and talents that made them nearly unstoppable.

I even thought about trying to break up this team from within. But once I really thought it through, I didn't think that would stop them. It would only delay the inevitable.

They'd come back together again. It seemed they were drawn to each other.

I had to keep a close eye on them.

They just couldn't understand what a wonderful thing was taking place. Sure, there had been mistakes along the way.

Those were to be expected. There was no perfect scenario here. Part of experimenting meant trial and error.

But I was ready to change the world.

And I wasn't the only one.

I had to keep moving forward. I had to cover up the things we'd done wrong.

And no one was going to stop me.

My mind continued to race ahead. To explore possibilities.

One scenario remained in my mind.

It was risky.

But in the end, it would be worth it.

I just had to figure out the perfect way to make it happen.

Andi Slade was the key. I needed her.

She would be perfect for what I wanted to do.

I would arrange it so she and I could have some one-on-one time together.

Then everything after that was going to change . . . for the better.

thirty-eight

AS DUKE WALKED into his old office building, memories filled him.

He really had enjoyed his time working with the Army CID. He never expected to be transferred to Alaska and to like being here. But America's Final Frontier had quickly started to feel like home.

After Celeste disappeared . . . that had changed. Duke had needed more time to look for her, and his job with the CID was demanding. It didn't give him the time he needed.

That was one of the reasons he'd decided to get out.

Starting his own business as a tour guide gave him flexibility. It let him earn money while still traveling to the area where Celeste disappeared.

Back then, it had seemed like a win-win.

But now . . . what if all of that was for nothing?

Duke knew he shouldn't think like that. But how could he not, considering everything that had happened recently?

The woman at the front desk was new and didn't recognize him.

He started to explain who he was and why he was here when the door opened and Sully stepped out. Sully with his tall, lean build. With his curly, dark hair that fell around his face. Brown eyes. Unconventional ways and affinity for eighties rock.

A grin stretched across his former colleague's face. "Duke McAllister. Good to see you. Thanks for coming in."

They went through the security procedures to get him into the back area.

"Working on a Saturday?" Duke asked as they strode down the hallway.

"You know how it goes sometimes with this job." Sully shrugged. "It's hard to have a life outside of it."

Duke knew that good and well.

He followed his friend into a small conference room, the two of them making small talk as they did so—updates on seemingly inconsequential things like work and dating.

Duke had been in here many times before, usually while questioning suspects.

It felt strange to be back again.

It almost felt like . . . he was going to be questioned.

His gut tightened at that realization.

Suddenly on edge, Duke tried to look casual as he sat down and stared across the table at Sully. "So, what's this about? What did you need?"

"Thanks again for coming." Sully's tone turned serious. "Actually, this meeting has to do with Operation No Name."

Duke's breath caught.

Operation No Name had been one of his biggest cases.

It had also been part of the reason why Duke decided to get out of the Army when he did. The pressure of the case and the fact that it was all-consuming was too much. Duke wanted more to his life than work, especially since he'd met Celeste.

She'd changed things. He'd thought she'd changed things for the best.

But maybe not. Now it appeared she may have been the one who turned everything upside down.

"What about it?" Duke shifted in the hard plastic seat.

"As you probably remember, there was some talk around the office," Sully started. "Especially when that file disappeared."

Duke's defenses rose. "I had nothing to do with that."

Sully raised his palms toward him. "I know. I'm not saying that you did."

Duke stared at his friend. He'd worked this job long enough to read between the lines. But he wasn't going to make this any easier for Sully than he had to.

His gaze locked on Sully's. "Then what exactly are you saying?"

———

ANDI WAS STILL TRYING to put all the pieces together as the team gathered.

Everyone, it appeared, was still trying to put the pieces together.

"If what you're saying is true . . ." Ranger started, his words coming out slow and purposeful. "Then these men you were following, who you thought were connected with Victor, are somehow also connected with Nursy Mercy—or, in the very least, the deaths at the hospital? That's assuming that Parsons' death was somehow connected with the deaths of those others while Celeste worked at Tanana Regional?"

Andi shook her head, her thoughts colliding inside her. She wasn't ready to claim that was the truth . . . but that was where all the signs seemed to point. "I know that sounds crazy. I do. But . . . that seems like a logical conclusion."

All this time, had there been a connection between what had happened to Celeste and what was going on with Victor? The coincidence seemed too great. Except . . . maybe this evil stretched wider and farther than any of them had ever imagined.

Maybe the connection wasn't a coincidence at all.

Andi squeezed her eyes shut, trying to make sure she wasn't seeing something that wasn't there.

But Ranger had seen the connection too.

"Are you sure this man was in one of the pictures?" Simmy blinked as she waited for the answer.

"I can't be 100 percent positive," Andi said. "But I have a pretty good memory. And I'm nearly certain I saw his photo."

"If that's true, then that takes all of this to a whole new level." Ranger crossed his arms, his body language shifting from curious to ready to act.

Andi nodded slowly. "You're right. It does. As soon as possible, I need to let Duke know."

thirty-nine

OPERATION NO NAME had been a doozy, Duke recalled as he sat in the conference room. Actually, doozy would be an understatement.

It had been a disaster—on more than one level.

The Army had been developing some cutting-edge technology in the use of artificial intelligence through an innovative new program.

Their hopes through the project was that fewer soldiers' lives would be on the line and technology would be at the forefront of warfare, which was really where things had been leading for a long time.

The Army had made some great strides in their work. The way they were now able to use drones in warfare as well as autonomous weapons and intelligence gathering was amazing.

But Duke and Sully had come on the case after it

appeared that someone in the military was selling classified information to a private buyer. Information about innovative ideas the Army wanted to try—but had some ethical dilemmas over.

The experiments being done involved electrical brain stimulation that would help program soldiers to act in a more predictable manner.

The idea was good, but the experiments had some devastating consequences, including brain damage.

Last Duke heard, investigators still hadn't figured out if the information had truly been stolen or who was responsible.

In the middle of that investigation, some test data they'd collected disappeared. Test data about ill side effects from some of the experiments they'd been running. Test data that had ultimately led to the program being shut down.

Their tests had proven that the whole program was too dangerous. Leadership knew if this information ever got into the wrong hands that someone could use the data for nefarious purposes.

Duke had been the last one to handle the files, but he'd never taken them from the office. He truly didn't know what had happened to them.

Since his name was the last attached, a few of his colleagues had suspected maybe Duke had done something with the files, at worst. At best, maybe he'd misplaced them.

Duke knew that neither of those things were true.

"Why are you bringing this up now?" He stared at Sully, not liking where this was going. "I already went through this explanation before I left the Army."

Sully cut to the chase. "I'm asking now because it has come to our attention that some of the technology our team was developing is now being created—and perfected—by a private firm."

Duke sucked in a breath. If that were true, the implications . . . they were far-reaching.

And dangerous.

Not just for him, but for the world at large.

That technology needed to be buried instead of developed.

Duke rolled his shoulders back when he remembered Sully was waiting for his response. "Okay . . . I didn't have anything to do with that."

Sully's expression remained unreadable. "I didn't bring you here to accuse you or to arrest you. I'm not even here to interrogate you. I just wanted to have a one-on-one conversation with you about what was going on so I can try to get to the bottom of this."

Duke wasn't sure he believed that. He knew how the game of tricky investigations was played.

This was Sully's way of making a move. Of observing Duke. Of feeling him out.

"I wish I had something I could tell you, but I don't." Duke shrugged. "I hadn't given much thought to this investigation in years. I assumed you guys had it handled."

Sully nodded slowly as he formed his next words. "I wanted to warn you that the heat may be rising on this. If there's anything you know . . ."

Duke's stomach tightened. "There's not. I promise you, there's not."

Sully stared at him another moment, almost as if trying to read his mind.

Duke kept his expression even.

First, Andi had nearly gotten herself killed by thugs Victor had hired.

Then Celeste was accused of murdering multiple people.

Now this old case was coming back to light.

Could things get any worse?

Truthfully, he didn't want to know the answer.

ANDI PACED THE CONFERENCE ROOM.

She didn't want to call Duke. She wanted to respect his wishes and wait for him to call her. But time seemed to be moving at a slow crawl.

What possible connection could James Parsons have with Victor? It didn't make sense.

"So correct me if I'm wrong," Ranger started. "But

what we're thinking right now is that somehow these mercy killings are connected with Victor."

Andi shook her head. "But that doesn't make sense. Maybe the death of this hospital administrator doesn't actually have anything to do with Nursy Mercy. After all, it would be risky for Kelly/Celeste to show her face right now when people are looking for her. So maybe James Parsons was killed by one of Victor's people. Maybe Victor wanted to set it up and make it look like Celeste was involved."

Ranger nodded slowly. "I'd say that makes more sense. Given the circumstances, I think it's safe to assume Victor knows that Duke and Celeste are connected. Therefore, if he wants to get in your head, then he could do something like this just to throw you off his trail again."

"This just feels like it's getting stranger and stranger." Andi paused and threw her head back in frustration. Her thoughts spun at such a dizzying pace that she was having trouble reeling them back in.

"What do you want to do?" Ranger cocked his head to the side as he waited for her answer.

Andi glanced at the time again. It had been an hour, and Duke still hadn't been back in touch.

One thing had been on her mind lately. But because it didn't connect with Celeste, Andi hadn't pursued it.

But with this new development . . . if Parsons' death was somehow connected with Victor . . . then the cases might be linked.

It seemed unbelievable. But when calculating people were involved, nothing was impossible.

She raised her head higher. "I know I mentioned to you all that I sneaked into the back of the van driven by some creepy guys and that Duke had to pick me up. I didn't go into all the details at the time, but these guys pulled up to this old, abandoned building outside of town. I need to find out what exactly they might have been doing there."

"Wait . . . how do you know it wasn't just an exchange or something?" Mariella remained where she was, the effects of her stomach issues making her less energic than usual.

"I don't know what was happening," Andi told them. "Until I go there, I'm not going to know why they picked that place to meet. I need to see what I can find out."

"I say we all go together." Mariella glanced at each of them. "I'm getting restless just staying here and doing all the admin work. I could use the fresh air. What do you think?"

Andi shrugged. "At this point, I say, why not?"

forty

DUKE SAT in his SUV after he left his meeting with Sully.

He couldn't believe their conversation. He didn't know what to think. To feel. To tell his teammates. If he should tell them anything.

He'd told Andi he would call her, and he would.

Just not right this second.

Right now, he needed to be alone a moment and think.

A thought circled in his mind.

A thought he didn't want to acknowledge.

A thought he certainly didn't want to speak out loud.

Because the idea seemed preposterous.

It didn't make sense.

Then again, a lot of things happening lately didn't make sense.

A memory had hit him when he was talking to Sully. He'd carefully concealed it from his expression, knowing Sully would pick up on it and want to drill him.

But Duke clearly remembered Celeste stopping by the office for lunch one day.

He'd given her a tour and introduced her to his colleagues.

Then he'd been called away a moment to talk to someone.

He'd left Celeste alone at his desk.

He'd been in the middle of working on Operation No Name—called No Name because the military wanted to make it disappear if necessary. He'd had paperwork out in the open.

Never in a million years would Duke think she might have taken any of that information.

She'd been a traveling nurse and the love of his life. She'd never given any indication she had an evil bone in her body.

So Duke had never once questioned if she'd taken the files.

Now, in light of everything that had been discovered, maybe Duke should consider the fact that Celeste could have somehow been involved.

But it still didn't make sense.

Why would Celeste open herself up to fall in love with him, get engaged, and come to Alaska to be with him, all while hiding the fact she was behind the mercy killings in California?

Then she'd picked up where she left off when she moved here to Fairbanks? In the middle of that, she'd stolen information on a secret military project?

None of the pieces fit.

In fact, maybe Duke was trying to make things fit that just didn't belong together.

More than one thing was going on here.

There had to be. It was the only thing that made sense.

That was why he couldn't stop thinking about all the pieces and possible connections. What if this turned out to be bigger than he, or anyone else on his team, could imagine?

What if there were more deaths involved than they knew?

Duke wished that Paul Brantley guy would talk to him.

He glanced at the time. It was almost six.

Maybe if Duke went by himself and explained who he was, he'd have a fighting chance to speak with the man.

Duke knew he should go back and meet with the rest of the club.

But he wouldn't be able to forgive himself if he didn't exhaust every resource to gain information.

He silently muttered an apology to Andi.

He would call her later and give her an update.

For now, he headed back to Paul's place.

He had to convince the man to talk to him this time.

———

RANGER DROVE AS THE TEAM, minus Duke, headed toward the abandoned building. Andi sat in the front giving him directions based on the best of her recollections.

She still wasn't sure this was a good idea.

What if they pulled up to something dangerous? What if they got caught in the middle of it?

At least, they had Ranger with them. He'd proven himself very capable as a former CIA agent.

Still, the last thing Andi wanted was to get Simmy, Mariella, or Matthew in trouble.

They passed the gas station where Andi and Duke had stopped and first heard the breaking news story about Nursy Mercy.

Where Duke had first seen Celeste's picture.

Where only seconds before that, she'd been certain he would kiss her.

Everything happened for a reason. She had to believe that was true.

She stared at the road up ahead. Andi knew they were getting closer.

A few minutes later, the lonely, gray building came into view. "That's it!"

Ranger slowed and drove past the three-story brick structure.

They studied it for any cars out front or on the side or in the back.

It appeared no one was there.

At the next turn, Ranger circled back around. This time, when he approached the building he pulled to the back of the place, just to be safe.

Then he stopped the SUV and stared up. "What now?"

"I think we should go inside," Mariella said. "See if we can find any clues about what might be going on here. Maybe those guys were just using the parking lot of this place to meet."

"But maybe they weren't." Andi raised her eyebrows.

"I don't know if it's a good idea if we all go in." Ranger shook his head, his lips pressed together in a tight line. "We don't know what we're going to find or how dangerous it might be."

"That's very true," Matthew said in the back seat. "I just looked this address up, and it turns out this place used to be a mental institution."

A shiver ran through Andi. "You've got to be kidding me . . ."

"Nope," Matthew continued, still reading something on his phone. "That's what this article says. It was in use for decades, but it shut down about twenty years ago. After a scandal."

"What kind of scandal?" Andi knew she shouldn't ask the question. Yet another part of her had to know.

"It says here it was shut down without warning after some mysterious deaths," Matthew said. "When investigators came in, they found several patients had been left behind . . . left in rooms where they died."

"What?" Andi glanced back at Matthew, unsure if he was being serious.

He stared at his phone and shrugged, not a glimmer of humor in his gaze. "That's what it says."

"That's majorly creepy." Mariella rubbed her arms as if chilled.

"Apparently, many people claim that 'ghostly activities' have been happening here since then," Matthew continued. "A lot of people—especially teenagers—like to sneak inside, almost as a rite of passage."

"Not to interrupt this campfire story, but you didn't, by chance, see if anybody has bought it since then, did you?" Ranger asked, stepping up to be the adult of the group.

"I'm trying to find out that information, but that's going to take a little more time." Matthew's fingers got busy on his phone again.

"I can't imagine why anyone would want to buy this place." Mariella stared at the building and shivered. "This is the perfect setting for a horror movie."

Andi didn't want to admit it, but those were her thoughts exactly. The place gave off a spooky vibe with its faded bricks, broken windows, and even several intricate cobwebs on the doorways.

So why here? Why had those guys come to this location to do whatever deal they'd done?

Unless they truly were trying to meet someone in an out-of-the-way location so they wouldn't be caught.

There was only one way to find out: by going inside.

Andi really wished Duke was here. She'd come to lean on his insight and understanding. She also felt safer with him around.

But he wasn't here, and they needed answers. Time was ticking away—and they didn't have any more to lose.

Besides, the longer they stayed in the SUV staring at that creepy building, the less she wanted to go inside.

One glance at Mariella's pale face told Andi she wasn't the only one to feel that way.

"Everyone ready?" Andi asked.

She didn't wait for an answer as she reached for the door handle—they might as well get this over with.

forty-one

DUKE MIGHT AS WELL GET this over with.

He pulled up to a stop at Paul Brantley's house again and lifted a quick prayer for wisdom and discernment. Then he climbed from his SUV and headed to the front door.

He knocked but heard nothing inside.

"I know you're home," Duke called through the wood. "I'm sorry to come back like this. I know you said you didn't want to talk. But you have answers we need. Answers that will help us stop a killer before another person ends up dead. I really need to talk to you. No strings attached."

Still nothing.

Was Paul okay? What if someone had been following Duke the last time he was here, and something had happened to Paul as a result?

Duke's muscles squeezed at the thought.

He started to walk toward the window nearest the door to peer inside and make sure the man was okay.

Before he reached it, the door opened.

Paul sat at the entrance in his wheelchair, his expression tight and annoyed. "When I saw you the first time, I had a feeling you weren't the type to give up easily."

"Thank you for answering." Duke kept his voice light but serious. "I promise you, I wouldn't have come back if this wasn't of life-or-death importance."

Paul stared at him another moment before sighing. He wheeled back and nodded behind him. "Come in."

Duke stepped inside and quickly glanced around. The place was cozy and clean, with minimal furniture and decorations.

Paul directed him to a beige chair, and then he wheeled in front of Duke.

"What are you trying to find out?" Paul wasted no time getting down to business.

"I'm here to ask about Compassion Mission," Duke started.

Paul's gaze instantly clouded. "I'm familiar with Compassion Mission."

This was a good start, Duke mused. "What can you tell me about them? No one else seems to believe the organization really exists."

"I'm not going to ask how you found out my name or my connection with them." He shook his head slowly as if bothered by the idea "I suppose that's really not important at this point."

"Somehow, you did hear about them though, right?"

He let out another sigh. "Someone from the organization contacted me by email. Said they were a startup company looking to help people in similar life positions as mine. At that point, I was feeling pretty low. Though I'm thankful to be alive, living like this definitely comes with its challenges. Before the wheelchair, I was an avid hiker, and I loved whitewater rafting and doing anything adventurous. A lot of that has changed since my car accident."

"I can only imagine." Duke shifted. "Not to be insensitive, but time isn't on our side right now."

"I understand."

Duke let out a breath. "So you got this email, and what did you think?"

"Once I started reading into the company, I was fascinated. They showed me some brochures of accommodations I knew could help me in my own house."

"Do you still have any of those?"

Paul shook his head. "I'm sorry, but I don't. I didn't think it was that important."

Duke fought a frown. Were these people trying not to leave a digital footprint? That was definitely how it sounded. Usually, people or organizations that did that had something to hide.

Paul glanced over his shoulder at his kitchen behind him. "The company is responsible for some of these updates. They made this into a smart home so I can operate things with just my voice. They installed shelves in my kitchen that can be lowered so I can reach things. Even my kitchen counter is low so I can prepare food for myself."

"That all seems very helpful."

"It really is." He paused. "But they were also doing some new therapies and infusions and—"

"Did you say infusions?" Duke remembered Ruby talking about her husband having an infusion of some sort.

Was that a link? Duke wasn't sure, but he kept that fact in the back of his mind.

"That's right." Paul nodded. "But we didn't get that far with things."

"What happened?"

"I was interested, but I didn't want anyone to know I was talking to these people. What if they ended up being kooks? If I got scammed? At least I could keep my pride. When I initially began talking to them, I agreed to meet— but only at the library, where I probably wouldn't run into anyone I knew."

"Did you actually meet with someone?"

"I did. A nurse named Celeste Dawson showed up."

Duke's stomach sank. Although he was unable to deny at this point that Celeste was somehow involved, the confirmation was still hard to swallow.

"She was kind and charming and said she wanted to help me. Said the company had gotten a grant that helped with expenses, so I didn't have to worry about any costs associated with their medical program. She told me there were several different ways these infusions could help, from controlling my tremors to pain management. They were even hoping it might give some people the ability to use their limbs again."

"All from infusions?"

"She said it was a little more complicated than that, but her colleagues called the treatment *infusions*. She said the procedure was simple and painless."

"But she didn't say what kind of infusions these were? If they were shots you'd receive every week or something else?"

Paul shook his head. "We didn't get that far."

"What happened next?" Duke held his breath as he waited for the answer.

His gaze darkened. "I initially agreed to participate. That's why I have the adaptations I have here at the house. But when they started talking about the medical aspects . . . that's when I got really cautious."

"Why is that?"

"It sounded like they were heavily into experimentation. A lot of the options they told me about seemed . . . unrealistic and unnerving. I told them I wasn't interested, that I didn't want to be a lab rat. Celeste didn't look happy with my choice. In fact, she almost looked desperate to get me to agree. She used all the classic sales techniques as if her life depended on my participation."

Duke wondered how that connected with everything else he'd learned so far. "Keep going."

"I'd declined and thought that was the end of the conversation. But I ended up hearing from her again and again. She kept trying to convince me to change my mind. I told her thank you, but no. I was always polite about it. However, she wouldn't back off."

Duke couldn't picture Celeste being like that. She'd been a kind, gentle soul when he knew her. "What did you finally do to get her off your case?"

Paul shrugged. "One day, she just stopped calling me."

"And you never heard from her again?"

"I didn't. I'm not sure what happened."

What had caused her to back off? Her conscience? Or something else?

"When exactly did this happen?" Duke asked. "Do you remember?"

"I do." Paul nodded with certainty. "Two years ago in May."

Two years ago in May? That was when she'd left to go hiking.

She hadn't really backed off.

She'd left.

"If she backed off and let you go on and live your life, then why all the hesitancy to talk to me earlier?" Duke asked.

Paul locked his gaze with Duke's. "Because now, after hearing that story on the news, I know what she really wanted from me."

"And what was that?"

"Celeste was trying to find new ways to help people with assisted suicide." His voice pitched higher as he said the words, almost as if he were both insulted and hurt by the insinuation.

"Did she ever even mention that to you directly?"

He shook his head. "I was at a pretty low point in my life but, no, that was never mentioned."

"So you think she was trying to convince people to let her help them die?" Duke needed confirmation before he could even begin to really wrap his head around this.

He held his breath as he waited for the answer to his stark question.

———

ANDI WATCHED as Ranger rattled the doors to the old mental institution.

They were all locked.

Even the ones at the back of the building.

But when he headed toward one of the windows and shoved it, it easily opened.

He stole a glance back at them. "I'm going in first."

"Be careful," Simmy murmured, lightly touching his arm.

He cast her a tender look, one full of unspoken conversations, and nodded.

The next instant, he climbed into the building and landed on the other side of the window.

Something crunched as if glass were beneath his feet.

Then he nodded at them to indicate everything was okay before going to unlock the door.

A rush of nerves swept through Andi as she waited. This entrance here at the back had probably led to a fenced-in area at one time. The remnants of barbed wire were scattered around the perimeter. The whole scene reminded Andi of a prison yard.

What would they find inside? Anything that would help them? Or was this just a wild goose chase?

They'd never know unless they did more digging.

A moment later, Ranger opened the door, and they stepped inside.

The stale air was chilly and smelled like dust.

Her gaze swept the place.

It had clearly been abandoned for a long time. In front of her were several industrial-style couches and chairs, now overturned and ripped. Lights hung from the ceiling, and graffiti littered the walls.

"Stay behind me," Ranger said, his muscles bristled and ready for action.

No one argued.

Andi pulled up the flashlight on her phone so she could see where she was walking. Even though there were windows, the sun had sunk behind the hills and trees in the distance. It was too shadowy for her to have a clear vision of what was in front of her.

Simmy stood close on one side of her and Mariella on the other. Meanwhile, Matthew took the rear, his phone in hand but not because he held a flashlight. It appeared he was locked and loaded, ready to look up anything they might have a question about.

"I don't know about you, but I get the impression that nobody's been here for a while." Simmy squeezed Andi's arm tighter.

"That's how it looks . . . over here, at least." Andi couldn't argue.

Ranger pushed through another door, and it opened to a hallway. Sheets of plastic hung from the ceiling covering a few doorways as if renovations were taking place.

Another larger door stood to the right.

Ranger opened it, and an eerie squeak cut through the air.

An office appeared, one redone with new carpet, new furniture, and creamy white walls. A filing cabinet stood in one corner, and a bookcase was being built near another wall.

A pile of papers rose on the desk, along with a stapler and charging cord.

This room looked markedly different than the rest of this side of the building.

Why would someone clean this room up? What were they using it for?

Andi paused near the desk and stared at a folder on top. She opened it and saw a medical file inside. There were blood results, X-rays, a medical history form.

The patient's name had been crossed out with a black marker, making it unreadable.

Was this leftover from when this place had been a psychiatric institute? It seemed too new.

She opened a drawer and saw more of those coin-sized metal discs she'd found in the back of the van. What were those? And why were those in a box in here?

Before she could look any further, Mariella let out a moan, and her hand went to her stomach.

"Mariella?" Andi whispered. "What's wrong?"

"I . . . I'm not feeling very good. My stomach . . ."

Andi's gaze went to Simmy, but she wasn't showing any of the same symptoms.

Mariella moaned again and bent forward.

Concern surged through Andi. Was Mariella sick again? Or was this a remnant of her original sickness? Maybe she should have gone to the doctor when she first started feeling bad.

Just then, tires rumbled in the lot outside.

Ranger glanced back again. "We need to get out of here. Now."

forty-two

"I THINK they wanted to experiment on people with nothing to lose," Paul continued to tell Duke as they sat in the man's living room. "I don't know any details of what those people were up to. But I didn't trust them."

"Those people?" Duke thought Celeste was the only person Paul had spoken with.

"One time when I was talking to Celeste, I saw a man waiting for her in the car." Paul raised his eyebrows as if to drive home his implication.

Duke swallowed hard and realized a lump had formed in his throat. "Could you describe this man?"

"Not really. The windows were tinted, but I could see enough to know he was tall with broad shoulders, so I assumed it was a man."

"But Celeste didn't give any indication who he might be?" All Duke could think about was, what if this guy was

William Ladak? What if he was in on this scheme, even before Celeste disappeared?

What if Duke and Celeste's relationship had never been real?

"Sorry." Paul shrugged. "I wish I'd seen more, especially knowing now what I didn't then. But at the time, the experience didn't seem consequential."

"It's probably good you refused to participate beyond the accommodations they incorporated into your home."

Paul nodded slowly, his voice cracking as he said, "Absolutely. Otherwise, I'm convinced I wouldn't be here right now."

His tone made it clear that he truly believed his words. That Paul thought Celeste's ultimate goal was to kill him.

But in that case, it wouldn't have been a mercy killing. That didn't fit what they knew so far about Compassion Mission and what Celeste had done.

So what sense did this new information make?

Duke was slowly inching closer to answers. But he wasn't there yet.

There were still too many holes in the path he needed to traverse.

Even though he didn't like the picture forming, he had to keep moving forward. Had to keep pressing for answers—even if those answers devastated him, and they had the potential to do just that.

For now, Duke didn't have any more questions.

He stood and thanked Paul for his time. "If you think of anything . . ."

"I still have the card you left at my door." Paul nodded toward the paper on a table near the couch.

"And the FBI—"

Paul nodded again. "I know I need to talk to them. I signed an iron-clad agreement with Compassion Mission when I began working with them, saying I wouldn't speak about the details or I'd be sued. Since nothing bad happened and Celeste stopped showing up, I decided not to report them. But if they wanted to kill me then, I can only imagine how much they'll want to kill me once they find out I ratted them out."

Paul's explanation made sense. Andi could probably shed some light on the legal aspect of the situation. But, for now, Duke had a little more to go on.

He climbed back into his SUV, ready to call Andi now and tell her the updates.

But her phone went straight to voicemail.

Straight to voicemail? Duke thought for sure Andi would be sitting waiting for an update.

The fact she hadn't answered . . .

That familiar sinking feeling dipped in his stomach.

Something had happened, hadn't it?

———

ANDI GRABBED Mariella's hand and pulled her deeper into the renovated office space.

Ranger had already stepped inside with Simmy, and Matthew was right on their heels.

As soon as they stepped through the doorway, light filled the hallway behind them.

Whoever was here was already inside the building.

And there was working electricity at this place. At least, in part of it.

Weird. Unexpected. Curious.

Andi didn't know what to make of all this.

Ranger directed them behind a tall bookcase angled away from the wall. Then he put his finger over his mouth, indicating they should all be still.

Andi felt so stiff she wasn't sure she could move even if she wanted to.

Who was here? What was this person going to do?

She wasn't sure it was a good idea that they'd stuck around to find out.

But right now wasn't the time to run.

This was exactly what she'd feared would happen.

That they'd be cornered.

That Simmy, Mariella, and Matthew could be in danger.

Andi and Ranger had known exactly what they were getting into. She wasn't worried about the two of them. At least, they could defend themselves. Well, Ranger more than Andi. But she was scrappy and at times too fearless for her own good.

But the rest of the gang . . . they weren't equipped for stuff like this.

Just then, Andi's phone buzzed in her pocket.

Andi didn't dare move.

Was it Duke calling her? That was her best guess.

Thankfully, no one else heard the vibrations. Andi only felt them.

She continued to hold her breath and listen.

Beside her, Mariella moaned again and bent forward.

"Mariella?" Andi whispered.

"My stomach . . ."

Oh no. Was the virus/food poisoning rearing up again? Talk about awful timing.

"Hold tight for a few more minutes," Andi whispered.

But Mariella's pale face did little to assure her that was possible.

Andi's thoughts continued to race.

If whoever had gone inside looked at the back of the property, they would see Ranger's SUV there. They might begin to search this whole place.

That would lead to trouble.

Footsteps sounded in the distance. More than one set.

How many people were here?

Were they coming this way?

She wasn't sure.

Then a door opened. Not just *any* door. The door leading to this room.

Andi exchanged a look with Ranger.

Then she prayed they would be invisible.

forty-three

DUKE TRIED to reach Andi again, but she still didn't answer.

Then he tried the rest of the team.

They didn't answer either.

His worry kicked into higher gear.

It was nearing eight o'clock. The sun was sinking closer to the horizon, and the air appeared grey with dusk.

It was a good thirty-minute drive back to Fairbanks, and Duke couldn't wait to share what he had learned with everyone else.

Most of all, however, he was concerned.

The best-case scenario was that he'd get back to the lodge and find the gang together doing some intense activities they couldn't interrupt. Yet he knew it was highly unlikely that was the case.

As he drove, his thoughts continued to race, putting together a better picture of what had happened.

This was what he knew so far.

Kelly Hanson/Celeste Dawson had worked as a nurse in California. She was somehow connected to the death of six people in Burbank.

She possibly feared getting caught so she'd fled.

Less than a year later, Duke had met her at a ski resort in Colorado, and she'd told him she was currently living in Denver. Sometime in between California and Colorado, she'd lived in Nebraska. Duke wouldn't be surprised if she'd lived somewhere else also. In fact, at one point, she'd gone by the name Ella Fischer.

When he'd first met her, it had felt like love at first sight. They'd begun to date and had fallen in love quickly. Shortly after, he was reassigned to work in Alaska.

Celeste had come to Fairbanks twice to visit him. The second time, Duke had proposed. Three weeks later, she'd accepted a traveling nurse assignment in Fairbanks.

He had never felt so happy.

He now knew that Celeste had moved to Fairbanks only to pick up where she'd left off in California, almost like murder was in her blood.

Had she purposefully wanted to come to Fairbanks? Or was she content to "bloom where she was planted," though the use of that phrase seemed like a stark contrast to what she was really doing.

If she came here on purpose, had she used him to get here? Was what they'd had between them real?

She'd most likely killed four more people. Then something must have happened to spook her. Perhaps Craig had discovered what she was doing. Maybe that would explain the bracelet belonging to Celeste that had been found at his cabin.

Then she'd made up that story about wanting to go on a hike at Gates of the Arctic.

Duke hadn't questioned it because he knew she liked hiking. But he had wondered why she'd refused to wait for the opportunity for him to go with her. Now it made more sense.

That was also at the time he was involved with Operation No Name. She'd possibly taken some of his files from that investigation, though he still wasn't sure why.

During the time Celeste was in Fairbanks she'd tried to recruit people she could "help" through Compassion Mission. Still working as a nurse, she'd continued her murder spree. But she had to have been working with someone else. Maybe that was where William Ladak had come into the picture. But why would a philosophy professor want to help Celeste kill people?

Duke hadn't put that together yet.

Apparently, if what Kyle and Paul said was correct, Compassion Mission was still in existence. It made sense. Celeste wouldn't have been able to do all this alone.

He would bet she'd never been working alone. Maybe

there was a whole team behind this, but Celeste was the fall guy.

Now that these murders had been discovered, Celeste was trying to cover her tracks. Perhaps that was why she'd killed James Parsons, the administrator at the hospital.

Duke let out a sigh.

That was all he'd pieced together so far. Some of his theories were based solely on assumptions and probabilities. But he believed he was on the right track.

He drove back to the Grayling Lodge and quickly hurried inside.

When he got to the conference room, it was empty.

His gut clenched.

The rest of his team was gone, and Duke had no idea where they might be or if they were in trouble.

———

"COME OUT, come out, wherever you are," a deep voice called.

Andi would bet the voice belonged to one of the thugs whose van she'd stowed away in.

Ranger glanced at the team, his look clearly conveying a silent message: don't make a sound.

Andi stole a glance at Matthew and Mariella. Matthew looked terrified with his wide eyes and wooden movements. Mariella still looked green around the gills.

The poor thing.

Andi wished she'd brought her gun with her. But it was stashed in a safe in the back of her car.

"We know you're in here somewhere." The man continued walking down the hallway, opening various doors, his footsteps thudding against the floor. Each step was slow and methodical as if he were enjoying this hunt.

The realization didn't make Andi feel any better.

The footsteps stopped.

A moment later, the man started whistling, the sound so casual that it was eerie.

Then the footsteps continued. Getting louder. Closer.

He was coming.

At any minute, he'd step into this room and quite possibly look on the other side of the bookcase.

That meant he'd see Andi and the rest of the team.

Ranger turned toward them. "On the count of three, follow my lead."

He said the words so quietly that Andi could hardly hear him. But his message was loud and clear: one mistake could devastate them.

The door creaked open wider.

There was another step.

Then another.

The man was in the room, she realized.

The next instant, Ranger pushed the bookcase. The heavy wooden furniture toppled over, crashing onto the floor.

A groan followed.

It had landed on the man, hadn't it?

"This way!" Ranger yelled.

They all scrambled around the bookcase, despite the man writhing and twisting as he tried to get out from under it.

At any minute, this guy's partner could come running. Andi had no doubt he'd have a gun.

They ran to the door and flew outside. Mariella moved slower than the rest of them, but Andi kept a hand on her arm and pulled her along.

Ranger's keys were already in his hands.

They practically dove inside his SUV.

Just as they pulled away, another man stepped out the back door.

Glared.

Raised his gun.

"Everyone get down!" Ranger yelled.

They all ducked as the man fired.

The back glass of Ranger's SUV shattered.

Mariella screamed.

Despite the chaos, he kept driving. And driving. And driving.

Soon the building and the gunman disappeared.

But Andi knew they weren't out of danger yet.

forty-four
Then

SHE DIDN'T KNOW what was happening.

The blackouts were coming more frequently.

So were the headaches.

Every time she considered asking for help, something changed inside her.

The next thing she knew, she was back at work.

Nothing had been addressed.

She only felt confusion, felt a disconnect between her mind and body. It seemed to be getting worse.

Nothing made sense to her, and it was almost as if she were simply going through the motions.

All the time.

Just the other day, she thought about walking away from this life. Leaving it all behind.

Then she was back at her house, and the idea seemed to be forgotten.

Then there was yesterday.

She'd blacked out again. When she came to, there was blood on her hands. On her shirt.

She didn't know why.

It wasn't her blood.

Had she hurt someone? She didn't think she had. Why would she?

Nothing made sense.

Her heart began to palpitate, pounding faster and faster until it was all she could hear.

She sat in the bathtub at her place, trying to find comfort in the warm water.

For a moment, she considered dipping low. Placing her head beneath the water.

Not coming up.

That seemed easier than living in confusion.

But she couldn't do that—for more than one reason.

Instead, she soaked up the warmth, dreaming of a different life than the one she was currently living.

A life that didn't feel like her own.

What was going on with her?

Her head pounded harder.

Harder.

Maybe she needed to go talk to someone.

Maybe she should see the doctor. Have a physical.

She rose.

That was what she'd do.

But just as she stepped toward the door, an electrical shock zapped through her.

Then her mind went blank again.

forty-five
Now

DUKE LOOKED up as a group of people walked into the lobby.

The breath left his lungs when he realized it was the rest of the gang.

They were back.

Based on their disheveled appearance, not all was well.

He met them halfway. "Are you guys okay? I was worried."

The glances they exchanged showed that everything was *not* okay.

He'd had a right to be concerned.

"Long story." Andi paused in front of him, dust in her hair. "But we're fine now."

His gaze stopped on Mariella, who looked pale as she grasped her stomach. "Even Mariella?"

"She's feeling sick again," Matthew explained. "The same thing she had earlier."

"Should you go to the doctor?" Duke asked.

Mariella waved him off. "I'll be fine."

Andi turned back to him. "How are you?"

Everyone gathered in the conference room and seemed to collapse around the table.

Duke took his cue and sat down as well. Then he updated them on what Sully had told him—not all of what he'd said but part of it, at least. He also gave them the update on Paul.

When he finished, Mariella told him about their adventure at what used to be a psychiatric institution.

Before she finished, the rest of the team joined in, adding their own details to the story.

Their experience at the old building was the last thing Duke expected to hear.

Those thugs had gone back to that building? What exactly was going on at that place? There was clearly more to the story.

While the gang talked, Matthew used his computer to research who may have recently purchased the building—if anyone. These guys might just be using the space because it was abandoned.

They still had a lot of questions.

It was getting late, and they were out of daylight. Anything else they'd want to do would need to wait until the morning.

"I guess we reconvene tomorrow?" Mariella asked.

"Wait a minute . . ." Andi said. "Wasn't Alpine supposed to make some type of announcement today? Did anyone turn on the news?"

"That's right!" Mariella's eyes brightened. "Not that it has anything to do with this case, but I *am* curious about what our investor is up to now."

"I'm on it." Matthew began typing more rapidly on his computer. A few seconds later, he turned the screen toward them. "It looks like we just missed the announcement about thirty minutes ago."

Then Matthew hit Play, and Duke braced himself for whatever Alpine had to say.

———

ANDI WATCHED as Alpine's face appeared on the screen. Alpine with his red hair and ruddy complexion. His disproportionate facial features. His heavy brow and sagging gaze.

He wasn't handsome in the traditional sense, but plenty of women were willing to overlook his less-than-attractive qualities when they realized how much money he had.

"I'm coming to you now with an announcement I've been sitting on for a while." Alpine stood on a stage, reminding Andi of Steve Jobs when he used to unveil new Apple products.

For a long time, Andi had thought of Alpine as someone who aspired to be the next Elon Musk: a tech genius and icon. This announcement only drove home that point. The wealthy philanthropist wasn't ready to throw in the towel, as the saying went, on his business ventures.

"My team and I have been hard at work for the past several years trying to develop products that will benefit all mankind," Alpine continued. "No more vanity. No more entertainment. I'm done with that. It's why I've dedicated my life now to helping the world become a better place."

For the next ten minutes he ran through all the good he'd done in the world.

Andi wished he'd hurry up and get to the point. She was halfway surprised he hadn't included their murder club in his list of good deeds since he'd heavily invested in them. He probably personally took credit for every case they'd solved.

"Today, I'm presenting you with Wavelength." He paused, looked at the camera, and then an icon of three black waves appeared on a screen behind him. "Wavelength is a revolutionary new technology that allows our brains to do what our body can't. What do I mean? Let me explain."

He paused again, all for dramatic effect, no doubt.

"Wavelength is a small, minimally invasive implant that will help our brains become virtual computers. Our thoughts to become action. Our willpower to practically become programable. This will help people with disabilities do things they once thought were impossible—because that's where it all starts. With a thought. With a *wavelength*."

Now he had Andi's attention.

That sounded interesting. Promising.

Maybe even scary.

Just twenty years ago, this technology was something only talked about in science fiction. But now, some of these ideas were beginning to become a reality. It had the potential to change people's lives.

Hopefully, to change people's lives for the better.

She prayed that was the case.

But when she looked back at Duke, she noticed his face had gone pale.

Did he know something she didn't?

———

WAVELENGTH? That technology sounded an awful lot like one of the ideas that had been explored through Operation No Name.

But it didn't make sense.

How would Alpine have gotten his hands on that information?

Duke's mind swirled.

"Duke?"

He looked up from the table and saw Andi staring at him.

The rest of the team headed to their rooms, leaving just him and Andi.

More than anything, he wanted to share his thoughts. To tell her about what had happened with the CID.

But he couldn't do that, no matter how much he trusted her.

"Something about that announcement bugs me," he finally said.

Andi nodded slowly. "I get that. That kind of technology could be dangerous."

"Very."

"It could also change people's lives for the better."

He dragged one of his shoulders up. "I can't argue with that either."

"So what's on your mind?" She turned to face him.

The words stuck in his throat. He wanted to share them.

But he couldn't.

"You think there's a link between Alpine's announcement and something else that's happened?" Andi continued.

"I don't know." His voice cracked. "Right now, I really don't know."

She stared at him another moment. "Maybe we should

both get some sleep. Maybe things will make sense in the morning."

"Good idea." He rose slowly, part of him not wanting to leave, not wanting to be alone with his thoughts.

But it would be better that way.

Because he had some serious thinking to do . . . but he didn't like any of the conclusions he was drawing.

forty-six

THEY WERE GETTING TOO CLOSE.

Drastic measures needed to be put into play.

I had hoped it wouldn't come down to this, but it had.

I already had a plan.

Involving Andi, of course.

She would never agree to it. Not that I'd ask her permission.

But in the end, this would be a beautiful thing.

One day she'd realize she was part of something much larger, a bigger picture. All thanks to me.

It was going to be glorious.

I had to admit, part of me was annoyed with the woman. She was a little too pushy and persistent for my taste. That would make it even sweeter when she realized she had been chosen.

From what I had observed about her, she wouldn't go down without a fight.

It was a good thing I liked a challenge.

Thrived on it, actually.

I glanced at my watch.

It was just a matter of time now.

Then everything would fall into place.

A grin curled across my lips.

And I couldn't wait.

forty-seven

THE NEXT MORNING, the gang met in the conference room.

Andi took a quick inventory of everyone.

Duke still seemed preoccupied with something he didn't want to talk about.

Mariella still wasn't feeling 100 percent. But she'd insisted she'd be fine and had refused to go to the doctor.

Ranger was talking via Facetime with his daughter while Simmy peered over his shoulder and grinned.

Matthew was already on his computer.

After everyone arrived, Duke asked if he could lead them in a short devotion and prayer since it was Sunday.

The team agreed.

Andi had come to appreciate these moments. In fact, she even looked forward to them.

Duke, though tough on the outside, had a deeper, more introspective side that intrigued her.

Today, he read Ephesians 4:22–24, which talked about putting off your old self, what belongs to your former manner of life and is corrupt through deceitful desires, and being renewed in the spirit of your minds, and putting on the new self, created after the likeness of God in true righteousness and holiness.

Andi liked the passage, liked the thought of becoming a new person.

Duke was certainly a testimony for how people could turn their lives around.

Everything they had going on had remained on Andi's mind last night as she tried to sleep. So many puzzle pieces floated out there, close to snapping together to form a complete picture. But they weren't quite all there.

If Andi felt this way, she could only imagine how Duke was feeling since he had a personal stake in everything.

Duke wrapped up with prayer. "Give us Your wisdom, Lord, to find the answers we need. Keep us safe under Your protection. Guide our steps. Open the eyes of those who need to see the truth. We thank You, Lord, for Your unfailing love."

His words sounded so sincere and earnest that Andi felt herself leaning into the prayer.

She'd once thought religion was for the weak, but that

had changed. Some of the strongest people she knew were ones who depended on sources greater than themselves.

After they finished, they jumped back into work mode.

Duke pulled out a map of Alaska—one he'd gotten from the brochure stand at the hotel—from his back pocket and spread it across the table. One area was circled in red.

He jabbed his finger in the middle. "The center of this circle is Gus's Gas. I figure if Celeste is in this area, she's got to be within an hour radius."

Ranger glanced up, a skeptical look in his eyes. "You want us to search that area?"

"No, it would be too much. But I want us to keep our eyes open. I think Celeste is close. Maybe even watching us now."

"Makes sense." Andi had felt watchful eyes on her for a while now.

She didn't think the feeling was because the actress Brianna had been hired to trick them. She truly believed Celeste was still in this area and that she was here for a reason.

She just had to figure out what that reason was.

"Wait . . . I had another idea," Mariella started, her voice weaker than usual. "Since Alpine is a leader in AI technology, I thought we could ask him to look into Compassion Mission for us. I wondered if he might be able to shed some insight on this case. Besides, I think he's chomping at the bit to help us. He'll probably be thrilled if we ask him."

Duke glanced at Andi, and she shrugged. She didn't think Mariella's idea was a bad one, but this was Duke's investigation. He should be the one to call the shots.

Finally, he said, "I guess it couldn't hurt."

Matthew stared at his computer, one he'd pulled out right after Duke said "Amen." "Uh, you guys. There's something you might want to know."

"What do you see?" Andi rushed, her thoughts racing.

"I've been keeping tabs on some things, and I get notices when certain people do anything online," Matthew started, his gaze still fixated on the computer. "It all started when I was triangulating—"

"Matthew, I appreciate the explanation, but forget about the oyster and get to the pearl," Duke said. "What did you discover?"

Matthew pushed his glasses up higher on his nose as he looked at them. "It's about William Ladak . . . I've been tracking his email address. Long story short, the IP address associated with his email just pinged."

"Where?" Duke's shoulders instantly seemed to swell with tension and anticipation.

"About twenty miles north of Gus's Gas."

Duke glanced at the map.

That was inside the radius he'd circled.

He wasted no time stepping toward the door. "I need to check it out."

Andi's pulse raced as she followed behind him. No way would she let him do this alone. "I'm going too."

"Want me to come?" Ranger placed his hands on his hips as he waited for his answer.

"Not yet." Duke paused near the door. "If you guys could talk to Alpine, that would be great. Maybe even call Gibson and let him know what's going on, just so we can keep him in the loop. But give me a thirty-minute head start first. The fewer people who are there when I finally find Celeste, the better."

Andi knew where he was coming from. He wanted the moment to be private, but he wanted to be smart also. There was no telling what kind of situation they might be walking into.

She was honored Duke hadn't asked her to stay here. She wanted to be there for him—even if seeing his reunion with Celeste hurt.

As Duke grabbed the keys from his pocket and headed out the door, Andi followed behind.

———

DUKE TRIED NOT to press the pedal too hard. But he failed.

With every second that passed, William Ladak could be on the move.

This was Duke's opportunity to find him, and he couldn't blow it.

To Andi's credit, she didn't say anything as she sat in the SUV beside him, her knuckles white as she gripped the armrest and stared straight ahead.

Fifteen minutes into the drive, she finally asked, "What are you going to say to Celeste if she's there?"

"I'm not sure." Duke had thought about it a million times. He'd come up with uncountable different scenarios.

Scenarios where they ran to each other and embraced.

Scenarios where he laid into her about the agony she'd put him through over the past two years.

Scenarios that were a combination of them both.

But, in the end, the words coming from his lips would be from his heart. They might be kind. They might not be.

He couldn't be certain until that moment.

"Duke . . ."

When silence followed, he looked over and saw Andi lick her lips.

She was about to say something she didn't want to say.

He braced himself for her words.

"What is it?" His words were edged with caution.

Part of him didn't want to hear it. But Andi was intelligent. He'd be wise to listen to her. And he *had* just prayed for wisdom.

"What if this is a trap?" she asked quietly.

He swallowed hard. He'd thought about that.

Why had the IP address suddenly pinged? Why now?

This could all be a setup.

But he needed to know for sure.

"If this is a trap," he started, "then the moment you realize that, I want you to run—fast and hard. I want you out of danger. Will you do that for me?"

She didn't hesitate before shaking her head. "Absolutely not. I'm going to be there with you."

Duke's throat tightened at the thought of something happening to her. "Andi . . . please. I don't want you to get hurt because of me."

"I'm not going to let you die because I'm too afraid to stand up to evil people. Like it or not, I'm going to be right there fighting beside you. Nothing you say is going to change my mind."

He swallowed hard.

Duke knew there was no convincing her to do otherwise.

And he knew with certainty at this moment that he'd be a fool to ever let this woman go.

forty-eight

TEN MINUTES LATER, Duke and Andi drove down a gravel lane leading to the address Matthew had sent them.

With every inch closer, Duke's grip on the steering wheel tightened.

This could be the moment all his questions were answered.

Or this could be a wild goose chase and a total bust.

As he saw the trees clear ahead of him, he pulled to the side of the road.

He didn't want to announce their arrival. The element of surprise would work in their favor.

Before he and Andi climbed from the 4Runner, he turned to her one more time. He needed to give her one more opportunity to back out of this.

But before he even said the words, it was as if she had read his mind. "I'm going with you."

He stared at her a moment. At her pale blue eyes that were set with determination. At her chin as she raised it stubbornly in the air. At her blonde hair as she raked it away from her face.

There was so much he wanted to say to her. But right now wasn't the time. He needed to get through this first.

Then he'd tell her all his thoughts.

He'd tell her that even if Celeste was alive and well he wouldn't go back to her. That he was in love with Andi. That he had been for a long time.

When he'd first met Andi he'd been confused. Been torn between obligation and hope. Between trying to do the right thing and heartache.

It had felt like a no-win situation.

Would Andi understand his tortured emotions?

He prayed she would.

But, first, he needed this resolution with Celeste.

He swallowed hard and nodded toward the clearing in the road ahead. "Let's go then."

They stayed near the trees as they walked closer to the location.

Andi had found a satellite image of the area on the way there, and it showed a small cabin on a lake.

As they reached the end of the lane, Duke lingered in the trees to observe the place.

Sure enough, a small log cabin rose beside a beautiful lake that reflected the snow-capped mountains standing boldly all around it.

The place was the picture of serenity, especially since the lack of wind today made the water look placid.

But Duke didn't want to feel a false sense of security.

Nothing about this situation was docile.

He continued to study the area.

An old Jeep was parked almost out of sight on the other side of the cabin.

A wheelbarrow and a shovel had been left near one of the cabin's walls. A small garden had been planted in an open area to the north of the house.

Lilies bloomed in a neat row in the flowerbed at the front of the house.

Lilies? They'd been Celeste's favorite.

Not only that, but Celeste had always loved gardening. Was this another sign that this truly was her place?

A clothesline stretched near the garden with shirts, pants, and dresses hanging out to dry.

Clothes that indicated someone was living here.

A man and a woman.

Possibly Celeste and William.

"You ready?" Duke glanced at Andi, knowing he couldn't put this off any longer.

Because that was what he was doing: putting this off.

Knowing that the outcome today could bring resolution or more heartache.

Andi stayed behind him as they walked toward the cabin. Duke had his gun in hand, but he hoped he didn't need to use it. Part of him still hoped there was a simple explanation for all this. Something innocent that would absolve Celeste of any wrongdoing.

But he knew how unlikely that was in this situation.

"Duke . . ." Andi called as they got closer to the cabin. "Look."

He followed the direction of her pointed finger and glanced across the lake.

A lone figure sat in a small boat rowing away from the cabin.

A woman.

Celeste?

Based on her slim figure and blonde hair, maybe.

Almost as if the woman had heard them arrive, she glanced back.

Duke's heart lodged in his throat.

Her face, though far away, came into view.

And he was nearly certain the woman was Celeste.

———

ANDI PULLED her gaze away from the woman on the lake and glanced at Duke.

She saw the emotions flashing through his gaze.

Hope. Anger. Confusion.

She looked at the woman in the rowboat again as she rowed farther away from them.

Celeste . . . the woman looked just like her photo.

It was almost as if she'd heard them coming and taken off.

Just in time to break Duke's heart again.

A burst of anger coursed through Andi. Duke deserved so much better than what Celeste had put him through—and was *still* putting him through.

Andi wanted to have a few choice words with Celeste herself.

But it appeared the woman had no intention of returning.

How was it even possible she'd known they were coming? They'd been quiet. Andi doubted there was any type of alarm system in place that they'd triggered as they pulled down the lane.

Which led her back to the thought that maybe this was a trap.

Her muscles tightened even more.

The lake was just big enough to make it nearly impossible for them to follow the shoreline and reach her. Plus, the terrain was rocky and steep at places. Without a boat themselves, they wouldn't be able to follow her.

Andi glanced at Duke and the torment on his face before murmuring, "We can wait for her to come back to shore."

"She won't come back." Duke said the words as if they were the absolute, undeniable truth.

But he was probably right.

Celeste had wanted to get away. She didn't want to be found.

Duke didn't pull his gaze from the woman, and Andi sensed he needed a moment.

"I'm going to check the cabin." Andi nodded toward it.

He didn't say anything, almost as if he didn't hear her.

She slipped away and prayed this wasn't a mistake. Prayed that William wasn't inside waiting for her with a plan of attack.

Her gut told her that wasn't the case. She didn't sense danger crackling in the air.

But she'd be on guard, just in case.

Carefully, she climbed the wooden steps to a large porch overlooking the water. Two rocking chairs sat to the side. By the door were two pairs of hiking boots—one large and one smaller.

Celeste's and William's?

Andi paused at the door. Contemplated knocking.

Instead, she twisted the handle and opened it.

She scanned everything within eyesight before stepping into the place.

A dainty, well-kept living room and small kitchen appeared.

Still no signs of danger.

She stepped farther inside, still remaining on guard.

Two mugs rested near the sink, a percolator beside them.

Andi paced toward it and gently touched the side with the back of her hand.

The coffee was still warm.

Two people had definitely been here recently.

Celeste was on the lake. So where was William?

Andi stepped beyond a small half wall and glanced at the living room. A massive stone fireplace stretched high to the A-frame ceiling. A leather couch faced it. Hand-maid crocheted blankets were draped over the back.

Someone had been living here for a while now.

Two years?

Had Celeste and William been together the whole time Celeste had lived in Fairbanks? Had this been their weekend cabin before they escaped from the city—and Duke—permanently a few months ago?

Andi had so many questions.

As she stepped closer, her gaze caught something on the other side of the couch.

A man.

On his back.

On the floor.

William Ladak, she realized.

She rushed forward and dropped to her knees beside him.

Her finger went to his neck as she felt for a pulse.

It was still there but barely.

She scanned him with her gaze. No visible injuries or blood.

So what had happened to him?

She patted his cheeks. "William . . . can you hear me? Are you okay? What happened to you?"

He moaned.

Why had Celeste left this man here to die? He clearly needed emergency help.

There was much more to this story.

For now, Andi needed to do everything in her power to help William survive.

She wished she was doing it simply because she was a good person.

But it was also because he had the answers she needed.

forty-nine

DUKE CONTINUED to watch as Celeste rowed farther and farther away.

On purpose.

They'd had direct eye contact, and yet she kept going.

The truth was, all this time he'd been looking for her, Celeste had simply been running from him.

She had no desire to be reunited.

Duke wasn't sure at this moment she'd ever loved him at all.

All this time he'd wasted searching for her . . . yet Celeste had left him no other choice. She hadn't broken up with him. Hadn't explained anything. Hadn't done the right thing by any stretch of the imagination.

Instead, she'd watched him suffer from a distance while never stepping up to make things right.

She'd fled to a cabin forty miles away with another man. She'd taunted Duke by showing up at his hotel. By leaving a note at Andi's apartment.

What he didn't know was why. Had their entire relationship been a lie from the start?

How could he have ever been so stupid?

"Duke!"

Duke snapped from his thoughts and glanced at the cabin beside him.

Was that Andi?

Where was she? Had he been so lost in his own thoughts that he hadn't heard her leave?

He chided himself.

As she called to him again, he realized she was inside the cabin.

He darted toward her voice. As soon as he burst through the door, he spotted Andi kneeling in the living room, something in front of her obscured from his sight.

"It's William . . ." she looked up and murmured. "He's barely alive."

"What?" Duke rushed toward Andi.

William Ladak lay sprawled on the floor, unmoving.

Duke knelt beside the man.

"I'm not sure he's going to make it," Andi said, her voice breathless.

Duke put his cheek close to the man's mouth. "He's still breathing."

He turned William to his side and tilted his head back.

"I have a satellite phone in the SUV," Duke told her. "Go get it and call for help."

Andi nodded and took off.

As she disappeared, Duke stared down at William. "What happened to you?"

Not that he expected an answer. But he'd love an explanation.

However, a bigger thought remained.

Had Celeste done something to him?

Suddenly, William's eyes barely opened. He blinked. Closed his eyes again.

Opened them just a slit.

"William, we're calling for help," Duke said.

The man grabbed Duke's arm, squeezing it with surprising strength. His gaze, though hooded, locked with Duke's.

He braced himself for whatever would happen next.

William parted his lips. Closed them.

Then he muttered, "She's . . . out . . . her . . . mind."

As soon as the words left his lips, he went still again.

Was he trying to tell Duke that Celeste had done this to him?

Or was it something else? Why were those the words William had chosen to say?

Duke wasn't sure, but he suspected William was trying to warn him.

Or was this just another ploy?

ANDI GRABBED the phone from Duke's 4Runner and made the call.

If there was any hope William would survive and give them any answers, then the man needed immediate medical attention. More help than she and Duke could offer.

The emergency operator promised to send someone right away.

Then Andi called Gibson and gave him the update. She didn't run that past Duke first. But she knew it was the right thing to do.

Gibson told her he was fifteen minutes out.

She started back toward the cabin.

Then she paused.

Slowly, she swiveled her head toward the lake.

The woman—she had to be Celeste—had stopped rowing. She'd turned the boat around and now stared at Andi.

The boat remained in place, almost as if Celeste wanted to say something to Andi.

Even though neither woman said a word—not that they could hear each other if they did—it felt like a thousand conversations were taking place.

What exactly was Celeste trying to convey?

Was Celeste trying to tell Andi that she knew Andi had stolen her man? That Andi had better back off?

Or was she passing the torch and saying he's all yours now?

Maybe it was even something nefarious.

A bad feeling gurgled in Andi's gut.

Finding Celeste now, at this very moment . . . somehow all felt too easy.

She and Duke had been searching all this time, and it just so happened that today was the day the IP address for William's e-mail happened to ping? And she and Duke had gotten here just in time to find William almost dead and Celeste on the lake rowing away from them?

Andi's thoughts tumbled inside her as she tried to make sense of what had happened.

But she couldn't.

Even though she knew she should get inside to check on Duke, for some reason, she couldn't turn away from Celeste.

The woman continued to face her, rowing in place so she wouldn't drift back to shore.

Why? Why was Celeste doing this?

Something was wrong. Andi was sure of it.

She needed to get to Duke.

She turned to jog back inside.

Before she took a step, something pricked her arm.

She reached for the spot, wondering if an insect had stung her.

But as she looked down, a shadow moved behind her.

She tried to scream.

But no sound left her lips or lungs.
Instead, her thoughts blurred.
Her muscles weakened.
She dropped the satellite phone.
Then everything went black.

fifty

DUKE LEANED toward William's face again. Listened.

He was barely breathing.

Duke turned him on his back and began doing chest compressions.

But nothing was happening.

He felt for the man's pulse again.

It was faint and fading.

"Come on," Duke muttered. "Hang on just a little while longer."

He glanced at the window.

What was taking Andi so long? Was she having trouble finding a signal? Finding his phone?

"Come on, William," Duke muttered.

He felt for a heartbeat again.

Still faint.

He continued doing compressions until William's heartbeat was steady.

Then Duke rocked back and let out a long breath.

What had happened to the man?

He glanced behind William and saw something that had rolled beneath the couch.

Duke pulled his sleeve over his fingers and lifted it up.

A syringe.

Had the liquid inside this nearly killed William?

Duke knew the answer.

Yes.

He rose, a bad feeling in his gut. Had William compromised Celeste's location? Had Celeste killed him for it?

Or had she purposely lured Duke out here for some reason?

He didn't know, but he needed to find Andi.

Now.

Duke stepped outside and glanced around.

Andi was nowhere to be seen. Where had she gone?

Had Celeste done something? It seemed unlikely since she'd been so far away.

His gaze veered to the water.

Celeste still sat there in her boat in the center of the lake, drifting out of reach.

She knew exactly what she was doing.

Unlike earlier, she faced him. Watched him.

Was she gloating?

Did Celeste know where Andi was?

A bad feeling gurgled in his gut.

He broke eye contact with Celeste and jogged toward his 4Runner, praying he would see Andi there on the phone with 911.

Instead, he spotted the satellite phone on the ground.

His breath caught.

He quickly scanned his surroundings.

But he didn't see Andi anywhere.

He never should have let her come out here alone. He should have known better, especially in light of everything that had happened.

He sprinted back to the lane, desperate to see if he'd missed anything.

But everything looked as it had earlier.

There were no signs of danger or of a struggle.

He returned to where he'd found the phone and glanced at it again.

His breath caught.

A second set of footprints marred the dirt near the device.

Big footprints—most likely a man's—with a pattern that reminded him of a boot.

And they weren't Duke's.

Someone else had been out here, just waiting for the right moment to grab Andi.

He snatched the phone from the ground. It hadn't locked yet.

Scanning it, he saw Andi's last call was to Gibson. Duke hit his number.

He answered right away. "Everything okay?"

"Andi's gone," Duke quickly explained. "Were you talking to her? Did you hear anything?"

"No, she called and told me what was going on. Then the call ended."

Duke's muscles tightened. What had happened after that?

"We're almost there," Gibson said. "Hang tight until we arrive."

Duke ended the call and put the satellite phone back in his SUV.

Then he scanned the woods again, looking for any signs of someone lurking just out of sight, ready to make a move.

He saw nothing.

With gun in hand, he began to follow the footprints.

He skirted between trees as he walked through the woods.

Then he came to another lane, one obscured by the trees. One with fresh tire tracks.

He realized with gut-wrenching certainty what had happened.

Someone had assumed Andi would come with him.

Then they'd waited for the right moment to grab Andi and take her away.

Celeste.

She was the one who'd orchestrated this.

This all had been a trap.

And Duke had fallen for it hook, line, and sinker.

———

ANDI'S EYES FLUNG OPEN.

A bright light blinded her, and she blinked.

Then she blinked again.

And again.

Where was she? Staring at the sun?

If so, why was she so cold? Why did her body ache? And her head?

She closed her eyes, unable to take the light anymore.

Her head swam as she tried to recall where she was.

But she couldn't.

Why couldn't she remember anything?

Then images began to haunt her.

She remembered seeing Celeste on the lake.

Feeling a prick.

Sensing someone behind her.

Then everything had gone black.

Now, here she was.

She forced herself to open her eyes again. This time, she turned her head.

Even with the light not directly in her eyes, all she saw were dark splotches from the brightness overhead.

She tried to make sense of things but couldn't.

Get a grip, Andi. Use your brain.

She sucked in a deep breath. The scent of dust and rubbing alcohol filled her.

Where had she smelled that scent before?

She couldn't remember.

She had to get up. Had to see where she was.

To get away.

She tried to turn.

Then she realized she couldn't.

Her arms and legs . . . they were bound to something.

She drew in another long breath, trying to keep her panic at bay.

She realized she was lying on something hard and cold.

As her hands reached out, metal pressed her fingertips.

The truth hit her.

She was on an exam table, wasn't she?

Or was it . . . an operating table?

More panic filled her, and she began to thrash, trying to break free.

Even though she knew it was no use, she continued jerking her arms and legs, trying desperately to get away.

Who had grabbed her? What were they planning to do with her?

As if to answer her, a shadow appeared beside her.

Even though Andi couldn't see, she sensed someone was with her. Had been watching her. Just waiting.

Then a feminine voice said, "You are going to be such a valuable asset to us."

Andi's blood turned ice cold.

She wasn't sure what that meant.

All she knew was the terror ripping through her was unlike any she'd ever experienced before.

fifty-one

AN HOUR HAD PASSED.

Maybe the longest hour of Duke's life.

It was enough time that the rescue squad had gotten here. They'd taken William Ladak to the hospital. Gibson and O'Brian had also shown up and taken Duke's statement.

Celeste . . . she'd disappeared. Maybe made it to the other side of the lake.

O'Brian said he would get a helicopter to search the area. Duke had a feeling they wouldn't find her.

She was behind this, wasn't she? Celeste had sent that email to lure them out here. She'd nearly killed William. Then she'd watched as someone grabbed Andi.

Grabbing Andi had probably been the ultimate goal. It was the only reason Duke could think of as to why Celeste would lead them here. To get Andi alone.

It was all calculated. Evil.

He swallowed hard.

All Duke wanted to do was to drive away from here. To search for Andi.

But he knew that would do no good. He wouldn't be able to catch up with her now. She could be anywhere.

He shouldn't have taken his eyes off her, not even for a minute.

But his grief over seeing Celeste and her betrayal had hit him hard. He'd been swept back in time. His own agony had superseded anything else.

That had been his first mistake.

A mistake he'd never forgive himself for.

Once Gibson and O'Brian finished questioning him, he grabbed his phone. He needed to tell the rest of the team what had happened.

Just as he wouldn't be able to forgive himself, Duke knew the rest of the team wouldn't be able to forgive him either.

He wouldn't blame them for that.

His heart was in his throat as he listened to the rings.

Finally, Ranger picked up. "You have an update?"

"There's something I need to tell all of you." Familiar dread pooled in Duke's stomach.

"Let me put you on speaker," Ranger said.

"What's going on, Duke?" Mariella asked, her voice still weak. "Did you find anything?"

Duke swallowed hard before starting. "Andi and I

found Celeste and William. But Celeste got away, and William nearly died."

"What?" Simmy murmured on the other line.

"I can tell you more about that later. But there's something else more important I need to tell you."

"Go ahead, because I have something to tell you also," Matthew said.

Whatever Matthew had to say, Duke couldn't force himself to care about it at the moment.

Only Andi mattered.

"When we first arrived, William was on the floor, fading fast. While I tried to revive him, Andi stepped outside to call 911. Then I went to look for Andi. But she was gone. Someone took her."

"Wait . . . what?" Mariella's voice rose in pitch at the words.

"I shouldn't have let her out of my sight." His voice was grim with regret.

"You couldn't have known what would happen," Simmy said. "It sounds like it was the perfect storm of distractions."

There was no way Duke would let anything that anyone told him make him feel better right now.

"Where would someone have taken her?" Ranger asked. "And why?"

"That's what we need to figure out," Duke said. "We don't have any time to waste. Gibson and O'Brian are here, and they're aware of the situation. They've put all their officers and agents on alert. But I have a bad feeling. Celeste had this planned."

"Maybe what I discovered will help," Matthew said. "I was doing some research, and I know you're not going to like what I have to say."

"Just tell me." Duke wasn't in the mood for guessing games.

"I won't go into all the details since I know time is of the essence," Matthew said. "But I found a link between Compassion Mission . . . and Alpine."

Duke's heart pounded in his ears.

Part of him had known this. Had feared this. Had been trying to put the pieces together.

"Tell me more," Duke said.

"I think Alpine owns and runs Compassion Mission, and I think everything has been done in secret because of some unethical practices they've employed."

Duke sucked in a breath. How could they not have seen this? He'd had his suspicions, but nothing like this.

"We need to talk to Kyle again," Duke said. "Maybe he can share some insight on this."

"I know where he's staying," Ranger said. "I'll go see what I can find out."

"Wait . . ." Mariella started. "One more thing you should know. I dropped my earring on the floor and when I crawled under the table to retrieve it, I saw something strange. It was a bug. Not like an insect. Like a listening device."

"What?" Duke's voice rose.

"It's true," Ranger. "We smashed it and checked the rest of the room. Didn't find any more. But someone has been monitoring everything we're doing."

His stomach tightened. No wonder they'd always been one step behind.

"I'm going to head back now," Duke said. "If I hear any updates, I'll let you know."

"We'll do the same." Mariella paused a second. "Andi's going to be okay, Duke. She's a fighter."

Duke knew the words were true.

But he couldn't shake the bad feeling in his gut.

All he could do right now was pray.

———

"WE'VE BEEN WAITING for you to wake up," the shadow beside Andi crooned. "It took much longer for that propofol to wear off than we thought it would."

Propofol? That was how she'd been sedated?

If the person who'd injected her had used it incorrectly, Andi could be dead right now.

She blinked, wishing she could see the face of the woman speaking with her. But the bright light above her made it nearly impossible.

"Who are you?" Andi sounded rattled, despite her attempt to be strong.

Was this Celeste? The woman somehow sounded familiar.

But Andi hadn't ever heard Celeste's voice.

"I know these bulbs can be blinding. Maybe this will help some." The woman moved the light away from Andi's face.

Andi blinked as she tried to adjust her gaze. All she saw were dark spots.

Then her vision started to clear.

A woman leaned over her.

But her hair was pulled back under a surgical cap. She wore blue scrubs. And a blue mask covered her face.

Between that and the spots Andi was seeing, she still wasn't sure who she was talking to.

"Who are you?" Andi's throat ached as she asked the question. "Why are you doing this?"

"It doesn't matter who I am. All you need to know is that we have a beautiful plan. We won't let anyone mess it up."

"What kind of plan?" Andi almost didn't want to know. But she needed to buy some time.

Needed to find a way to escape.

However, she was at this woman's mercy right now. No matter how much Andi pulled and tugged, there was no way she was getting out of the thick leather restraints at her wrists and ankles.

"You're about to find out." The woman's voice sounded eerily calming and soothing.

"You can't tell me in advance?"

"Sometimes I think it's better if my test subjects don't know what's about to happen."

"Test subjects? You're experimenting on me?" Fear shot through her.

"This is exactly what I'm talking about. When you know a tiny bit of information, you freak out. It's best you stay in the dark. If you knew any details, you might wet yourself because you'd be so terrified."

Andi sucked in a breath. She didn't like the way that sounded. This woman was already starting to terrify her.

She glanced around, hoping she might be able to see more of her surroundings. But she couldn't. "Where am I?"

"It's not important." An edge of irritation crept into the woman's voice.

It was important to Andi.

Would her friends ever find her? Would she ever go on any more adventures with the murder club? Would she bring any more killers to justice?

Then the truth hit her.

Andi knew where she was.

The thought of her friends had sent her reeling back in time.

Reeling back to when she and her friends had gone inside . . . the old psychiatric institution.

She and the rest of the team had only gotten as far as that office before that man had found them. But Andi knew part of the building had been renovated and restored.

Someone was using that renovated space for their nefarious deeds.

Deeds like this one.

Whatever *this one* was.

"A lot of times, I'm generous and put people under when I do this. But I thought it might be more fun if I kept you awake." The woman held up a scalpel and watched it glimmer under the light.

Andi's throat went dry. "You don't have to do this."

Even though Andi couldn't see the woman's lips because of the mask, Andi felt certain she was smiling as she said, "I know. But I want to."

Then the woman stroked Andi's hair before running a sharp fingernail down the center of her scalp.

Andi's head swirled as the truth began to sink in.

Whatever this woman was planning . . . it involved her brain.

fifty-two

DUKE'S HANDS gripped the steering wheel so hard his knuckles ached. But he had no time to waste as he headed down the road, traveling entirely too fast.

The team was still on the other line.

"Tell me what you know about Alpine's connection to Compassion Mission," Duke said.

"It was covered up really well," Matthew said. "So well that I wasn't even sure what I found was real."

"Keep going." Trees blurred past as Duke sped down the road back toward Fairbanks.

"I found some old correspondence someone tried to hide on the dark web concerning Compassion Mission. It took hours for me to search all of it, but in my gut I knew it was urgent. I stayed up most of the night working on it. This email conversation was between two people who wanted to quit but feared for their lives if they did. I looked up their names. They're both dead now."

"What?"

"Tragic accidents," Matthew continued. "However, one of them used Alpine's name in their correspondence."

Duke's thoughts raced. "Alpine did just announce that new tech he was developing. Wavelength. Isn't that what he called it? Have you done any research into that?"

"As a matter of fact, I have," Matthew continued. "Brain stimulation therapy has been around for a long time."

"How's it usually used?"

"Great question. There's transcranial magnet stimulation, which uses magnetic fields to treat obsessive-compulsive disorder, electroconvulsive therapy that involves electrical currents to treat depression, and deep brain stimulation that uses electrodes that are surgically implanted to treat Parkinson's, epilepsy, or tremors. None of those are cleared by the FDA, however. There are some advocates who think this could change the lives of hundreds of thousands of people who suffer from various ailments and disorders."

"Okay . . . so that's what this is about?" Duke squinted as he tried to read between the lines.

"Just to give you a little more history, in 1991 this guy developed a brain computer interface—known as a BCI—that allowed a man to move the cursor on his computer only using his brainwaves. Pretty amazing, right? The technology has come a long way since then, even allowing people to control robotic limbs."

Compassion Mission, a company that wanted to help the disabled.

The mention of infusions.

New technology involving an implant placed in a person's brain to help them with everyday tasks . . . in theory. In the wrong hands . . . that technology could be deadly.

Duke didn't like the picture forming in his mind.

There was so much more to this than they had initially assumed, wasn't there?

Another thought hit him. "That old psychiatric building you guys went to. Did it seem like anything might be set up there as a place they could be doing some of these experiments?"

"There was one room that had been renovated into an office," Ranger said. "But that's as far as we got."

What did the rest of the place look like? What were the thugs doing there? Clearly, it wasn't construction work.

"I think we need to check out the rest of that building," Duke said. "I'll head that way now."

"I'll meet you," Ranger said. "Do you want us to call the FBI or Gibson?"

"They're at that cabin now and are at least forty minutes out. We'll get there before they do. I'll let them know myself."

"Sounds like a plan," Ranger said. "We'll meet you there."

Duke ended the call.

He hoped, if his theory was correct, that he got where he needed to go before anything devastating happened.

Andi . . . please be okay. Please . . .

"I DON'T UNDERSTAND why you're doing this," Andi said as she stared at the masked figure above her.

Who was this woman?

Could Celeste have gotten here this quickly? Since Andi had gotten here, then it seemed like a safe assumption. Besides, she didn't know how long she'd been out cold. It could have been hours.

"We're doing this because we want to help people." The woman tilted her head, almost as if patronizing Andi.

"By experimenting on people who don't want to be helped?"

"We did the experiments first on people who *did* want to be helped." The woman continued playing with the scalpel and studying it under the light.

Andi's throat went dry as she imagined the surgical instrument slicing the top of her head. "And what happened to those people?"

"Unfortunately, things didn't work out for them."

The woman shrugged. "We need more test subjects, and you have been chosen for reasons I'm not privy to."

For reasons she wasn't privy to? So none of this was by chance? Each victim had a reason to be a victim?

Sweat spread across Andi's forehead. "There's a better way. Protocols to follow. Rules are set in place for these kinds of things."

"What makes you think these experiments have been approved by any agencies?" The woman moved behind her.

The next instant, Andi felt something stretch against her forehead.

A strap pulled across her skin, pressing her head in place.

It tightened until she could no longer move her head.

Panic thrashed inside her.

"No!" Andi tried to move but couldn't. "You won't get away with this."

The woman began playing with her hair again, pushing it back in a soothing motion. "Oh, sweetie . . ."

Andi wanted to scream, to crawl out of her skin and run away. But she couldn't.

She was trapped.

If this woman wanted to cut into her head and experiment on her brain then she would. If Andi continued to resist, that might only cause her more pain.

Yet she couldn't give up.

Maybe she could keep the woman talking. Andi was all out of other ideas.

She forced herself to swallow and take a deep breath. "So you're doing this so you can help people?"

"Of course," the woman crooned as if she were about to give Andi a fresh set of highlights instead of performing brain surgery.

"Not so you can make money?"

"Money isn't everything."

"What about power and control?" The thought slammed into Andi's head with absolute clarity. "If you can help people control their actions, then you can also control powerful people. You might even be able to manipulate them into doing things they wouldn't normally do."

The woman stopped stroking her hair just for a split second, almost as if Andi's statement had taken her by surprise. "I don't know what you're talking about."

"But I think you do," Andi said. "Even if you're coming into this with pure motives, that doesn't mean that everyone who works on these experiments will. It doesn't mean this technology won't get into the wrong hands, maybe even into the hands of your boss, am I right? Because you're not really the one behind all of this, are you?"

"Stop trying to get in my head." The woman started to stroke Andi's hair again. "Speaking of getting into people's heads."

The woman reached over and picked something up, holding it above Andi's head.

Andi gasped when she saw the coin-sized disc—just like the ones she'd seen in the back of the van.

Those had to be the implants.

Her limbs began to shake uncontrollably. But she couldn't let fear get the best of her.

Not if she wanted to survive this.

Andi licked her lips. "I'm just trying to talk this through. I can't go anywhere. I'm trapped. So I might as well understand."

"You're trying to change my mind!" The woman's voice pitched higher.

"Of course, I am. You're going to implant something in *my* brain."

"I get it. You're scared. If it makes you feel any better, I don't have to cut through the skull. We've perfected the procedure. The implant goes just beneath the skin, and it works just as effectively at sending information from the brain to a computer."

"I'll have it taken out."

"We'll program it so you won't even remember it's there."

Andi's blood went ice cold. That was how they were getting away with all this, wasn't it? By erasing people's memories that this had ever happened.

The idea . . . it was diabolical. And dangerous. And worse than Andi could ever have imagined.

In the wrong hands . . .

Political leaders could be controlled. Business owners. Cops. Judges.

Andi shivered.

"This could change the world as we know it," Andi whispered.

"Oh, we're definitely going to change people's lives," the woman agreed. "Starting with yours."

"I don't want my life to be changed." Andi jerked against her restraints again, even though she knew it wouldn't do any good.

"I'd say I'm sorry, but I'm not. Not really. But I *will* say thank you for your sacrifice."

Then the woman took the scalpel, and Andi felt the first prick of it against her scalp.

fifty-three

DUKE PULLED up to the old psych institute.

He didn't see any other cars around. Did that mean no one was here? Had his theory been wrong?

He couldn't be sure.

He only knew he needed to get inside and see if Andi was there. This place was the only location that made sense. He wasn't sure about all the connections and how everything tied together quite yet. But he knew enough to know he needed to find Andi.

He wanted to keep the element of surprise. He found a small opening in the woods and parked his SUV there.

As he did, he saw another vehicle was already stashed there.

Someone else *was* here. Probably more than one person.

But his team hadn't arrived yet. He knew he couldn't

wait very much longer. If he did, that difference in time could mean the difference in Andi remaining alive or being killed.

He crept to the front of the building and tugged at the door.

It was locked.

He continued to creep around the front, peering in the windows. From the outside, it looked as if the sun was reflecting off the glass. But the truth was most of the windows had been blocked with sheets of black plastic.

Someone didn't want other people to see what was going on inside.

How had Compassion Mission gotten people to come here? Had they all been kidnapped? Forced here against their will?

Or had they been lured here? Tricked into taking part in some kind of experiment?

Duke could only assume that was what had happened. One look at this building, and anyone in their right mind would run away.

Unless those in charge had somehow distracted their victims. Thought of a different way to get them inside. To get them to a room that, from the inside, appeared professional and reputable.

Duke wasn't sure. He'd figure that out later.

He reached the back of the building and saw an open window.

Carefully, he climbed inside and paused.

The room looked as if it used to be community space at one time. Now it was all overturned couches, knocked-over chairs, and sheets of plastic.

He headed to his left and quietly opened a door there. He crept down a hallway, trying to remember everything the team had said about when they'd been here.

Speaking of the team . . .

He glanced at the time. They should be here at any moment, along with Gibson.

Good. Duke needed backup.

For now, he continued to move forward.

Duke reached another door and paused. Then he twisted the knob.

An office stood on the other side, one that appeared very professional and up-to-date.

He was getting closer to answers, he was sure of it.

There was another door on the other side of the office.

He crept toward it and opened it.

But just as he took a step inside, a shadow sprang at him.

———

ANDI HELD her breath as pain sliced through her skin.

She started to cry out. But she didn't want to give this woman a moment of satisfaction.

She gritted her teeth instead.

Then a noise sounded in the distance.

Andi wanted to raise her head. To see what was happening. But she couldn't.

Even if she could, it might only cause this woman to slip up and cause more damage.

More damage? Was that even possible?

At least the noise had bought her more time.

The woman had stopped.

Listened.

She let out a *hmmm* before setting the scalpel on the metal tray beside the bed. "I'll be right back."

Andi watched as the woman left.

A sharp pain from the cut screamed at her. She sensed blood dripping through her hair. Moving only her eyes, she saw the tray.

From what she could tell, it was a good six inches from the operating table.

But what if she somehow shifted the table she lay on closer? Was that even possible?

She wasn't sure.

Using all her strength, she swung her weight to the right.

Maybe it was her imagination, but the operating table felt as if it budged just slightly.

If she could only move it a little bit more . . .

She gathered all her strength again and threw her weight to the side.

The table moved a little more.

This might be her only chance to get out of this situation.

Andi kept trying. And trying. And trying.

Finally, the table shifted enough that the tips of her fingers touched the metal tray.

She sucked in a deep breath, trying to remain calm.

She felt for the scalpel.

Finally, her fingers circled it.

The straps around her wrist were leather. It would take some work to saw through them, but it was possible. She prayed she had enough time.

If things worked out . . . maybe she could cut through these straps holding her down.

Maybe she could get out of here before the unthinkable happened.

fifty-four

DUKE THREW his shoulder into the guy's chest and shoved him away.

It was one of the thugs he'd seen with Andi in the van.

The man grunted.

Then Duke saw the knife in his hand.

As the man lunged at him, Duke reached for the weapon.

He brought his knee up.

Jammed the man's arm down on his leg until he heard a crack.

The man groaned.

But he didn't back off.

The thug seemed to have an adrenaline surge and charged at Duke again.

This time, Duke was ready.

He threw his shoulder into the attacker again. This time, he kept going.

He rushed forward until the guy hit a wall.

And he hit the wall hard.

The thug groaned again before clutching his arm, sinking to the floor, and closing his eyes.

He wasn't going to be any more trouble.

Just as Duke took a step back, a woman entered the room.

A woman wearing full surgical garb.

Duke could only see the woman's eyes.

Familiar hazel eyes.

Even though she wore a mask, Duke knew she was glaring at him.

"You should have never come," she sneered.

The next instant, she reached into her pocket and pulled out something.

A syringe full of a white liquid.

Then, she dove toward him, determined to plunge the needle straight into his neck.

———

ANDI CONTINUED to saw through the leather.

She *had* to do this. Failure wasn't an option right now.

But the task felt impossible. For every small slice into the leather, her skin felt as if it were also being sliced. A burning sensation marred her wrist. Blood oozed from her head.

But she had no choice except to keep going. This was her only hope.

Please, God. I know You and I have had our ups and downs. But I want what Duke has. I want to keep growing closer to You. Please, don't let things end this way. I'll do better. I promise.

Nothing like last-minute bargaining. But Andi was too desperate to even care.

Besides, she meant the words. She really *did* want to do better.

Unfortunately, it had taken this moment for her to realize it.

A few minutes later, something snapped.

Andi raised her arm.

It worked!

The scalpel had cut through the leather.

Victory flooded her.

She'd done it!

The bind was broken. *Thank You, Jesus!*

But she had to get her other arm and her legs free. Otherwise, she'd still be a sitting duck.

Before she could move her hand and try to undo the other strap, the door opened.

Andi quickly hid the scalpel beneath her arm and stilled.

She hadn't had time to get the other cuff off. But she could use this scalpel as a weapon.

Andi waited, trying to seem as if nothing had happened.

She needed the element of surprise to be on her side right now.

"I'm coming in to keep an eye on you until the nurse gets back," a deep voice said. "Let me inspect the work she's already done."

A man? Who was he?

Was he the head honcho? The brains behind all of this?

She didn't know.

All she knew was that the timing needed to be just right.

So she waited, instead murmuring, "Let me go."

"I'm sorry," the man said. "But that's not a part of our plan. Never, ever was it part of our plan."

"Who are you?" His voice sounded vaguely familiar. But where had she heard it before?

She couldn't place it.

Before the man could touch her head, she flung her arm up, scalpel held tight between her fingers. She sliced the blade through the air.

The man stepped back. "Whoa . . . didn't see that one coming. Nice try."

He slapped her hand, and the scalpel fell to the floor.

No!

An urgency unlike she'd ever known filled her.

She reached for the tray again.

Grabbed the first thing her fingers found.

Scissors.

Without hesitation, she plunged the weapon behind her.

The blade implanted in the man's neck.

He let out a curse. "You little . . ."

Then he lunged toward her.

As he did, his face came into view.

Kyle . . .

He'd been a plant, hadn't he? He'd only come forward as a whistleblower to throw them off the trail. To offer false information.

A surge of anger rose in her.

As Kyle snatched the scissors from his neck, he lifted them above his head. "I'll teach you a lesson."

Andi gasped as she braced herself to feel the oncoming pain.

fifty-five

DUKE HEARD the commotion in a nearby room.

Was that Andi?

Before he could think about it, the woman in front of him came back into focus.

Her face was covered with a mask and a scrub cap.

But her eyes flared and flickered, something twisted lurking deep within her soul.

As the woman launched herself at him, he grabbed her arm and twisted it.

The woman yelped. The needle fell to the floor.

But Duke didn't let go.

In one motion, he whipped her arm behind her, freezing her in place.

She let out another cry. "Let me go!"

That voice . . . he'd heard it before. He didn't have the chance to figure out where.

Instead, he grabbed a zip tie from his pocket and secured her hands behind her. Then he hooked the zip tie around her wrists to a pipe coming from the wall. He didn't want to worry about this woman getting in his way again.

"You can't stop us!" the woman yelled, still staring at him with those wild eyes.

Duke stared at her a moment, lasers coming from his gaze. Then he ripped the mask from her face.

He blinked. "Evelyn? You were behind this?"

She snarled. "Let me go!"

He didn't have time for this anymore—especially when he heard the cry from the other room.

He darted toward the noise and burst through the door in time to see Kyle standing with scissors raised above him.

No, raised above *Andi*.

Ready to plunge them into her.

In a split-second, Duke grabbed his gun.

Aimed.

Called, "Don't do it!"

Kyle paused. Looked up. Hesitated.

Then, with a smirk, plunged the scissors toward Andi's throat.

Duke pulled the trigger, and a bang filled the air.

Kyle stumbled back, the scissors clattering to the floor. Blood spread across his chest.

Duke held his breath as he waited.

Then Kyle collapsed.

Duke shoved his gun back into his waistband and rushed toward Andi.

Was he too late? Had they already implanted something into her? Harmed her in some other way?

He reached her, quickly kicking the scissors out of Kyle's reach—just in case.

Then he shoved the overhead light, adjusting it so he could see Andi.

She blinked but stared back at him, her head unable to move because of the strap across it.

His heart seemed to stop.

What had they done to her?

"Duke?" Her voice cracked as she said his name.

He cupped her cheek. "You're okay? Am I too late?"

His eyes flickered to the blood on the back of the table.

No . . .

What had they done to her?

"They didn't get very far," Andi murmured, her eyelids drooping.

How much blood had she lost?

He quickly undid the strap around her forehead, then the remaining bands around her wrist and ankles.

As soon as she was free, he pulled her into his arms, anchoring her to him.

"I was so worried," he whispered.

She clung to him. "You got here right on time. You always do."

Duke wanted to be there for her always. To get there right on time.

In fact, he never wanted to let her go.

If he had any say in it, he wouldn't.

Andi suddenly stiffened as if a memory had hit her. "Duke, there was a woman . . ."

"I took care of her," he murmured. "You should be safe now."

As he said the words, someone stepped into the room.

He stiffened, worst-case scenarios rushing through his mind.

Then he turned.

He released his breath when he saw Ranger standing there.

His fingers gripped Evelyn's bicep as the woman continued to snarl.

"You recognize her?" Ranger asked. "She nearly broke her wrists trying to get out of the zip ties."

"She's Evelyn, Celeste's friend from the hospital." Duke stared at her in disgust and shook his head. "How could you do this?"

"We're on the cusp of doing something wonderful that can help hundreds of thousands of people. We just need to tweak things. This was the perfect location for us to continue carrying out our experiments."

"Experiments that included Celeste?"

Evelyn didn't say anything. But Duke knew the answer.

Yes, the plan had included Celeste.

All the pieces wanted to come together.

But they didn't.

Not yet.

All Duke wanted to focus on at the moment was Andi and making sure she was okay.

Before they could talk anymore, sirens sounded outside. A moment later, police flooded the room.

Duke held Andi closer, vowing to never let her go.

AN HOUR LATER, Andi was at the hospital.

Duke had come with her. In fact, he hadn't left her side. Even as doctors stitched her up. Took her blood for a tox screen. Looked into her pupils.

She was forever grateful to have him with her.

In fact, she wasn't sure she'd be able to get through this alone. Everything overwhelmed her. Her head was still spinning. Her stitches stung.

Probably three hours at the hospital had passed before Andi and Duke finally found themselves alone.

Duke stood beside her bed, clutching her hand in his. He wouldn't stop staring at her. Deep emotions swirled in his gaze.

Andi licked her lips, knowing without a doubt there was something she needed to say.

She'd prefer to have this conversation after she'd showered. When she didn't have dried blood in her hair and on the collar of her shirt. When she looked and felt presentable.

But she couldn't wait a moment longer.

In fact, maybe she'd waited entirely too long.

"You came for me," she murmured as her gaze burned into his.

He leaned close, his eyes hazy with emotion. "Of course I did."

The words sounded raspy as they left his lips. This had been a lot on him also—on many different levels.

"You could have stayed at that cabin where we saw Celeste so you could eventually talk to her. You didn't."

He shrugged. "I'm not sure of everything that's going on with Celeste. But what the two of us had between us . . . it's over. It's *been* over. I just needed some closure, and I've got that now."

Andi's heart leapt into her throat. "I'm glad you got the closure, but I'm sorry it played out the way it did. Have authorities caught Celeste yet?"

Duke shook his head. "If they have, I haven't heard. By the time they got a helicopter out there, she was gone. They're trying right now to search on foot with the help of a couple of canines."

"They planted a chip in her brain, didn't they?"

He grimaced. "Most likely. My guess is that they wanted her to take the fall for this. They set her up."

"So who knows which of her actions were by her own choice or were forced upon her?"

"We may never know for certain. From what I've heard, the implants didn't work for many people. They had terrible headaches and their mental status deteriorated quickly. Instead of risking being caught, these patients were given curare and considered collateral damage."

"That's terrible." Andi shifted on her bed, her head beginning to throb again. "What about William?"

"I heard he's stable. The medicine he was injected with didn't have time to fully do its work when we found him. First responders were able to revive him and keep him alive while he was life-flighted here."

"That's good." A lump formed in her throat as she continued to gaze at Duke.

In the six or so months they'd known each other, they'd been through a lot. In fact, they'd been through enough experiences that their friendship had been tested time and time again.

They'd had some struggles, but they'd always come out stronger.

Somehow, it felt like their initial meeting and all their subsequent time together had been meant to be—for more than one reason.

She squeezed his hand. "I can't believe this all might be over."

He carefully lowered himself onto the edge of the bed and continued to peer at her. "I'm actually hoping this might all be beginning."

Her pulse quickened. "What do you mean?"

He swallowed hard, but his gaze never left her. "Andi, I've loved you for a long time. Everything that's happened . . . it only confirmed that for me."

Her heart leapt as joy filled her. She took a deep breath, not wanting to read more into his statement than she should. "Is that right?"

"I have no doubt."

Their gazes locked with each other's.

The next instant, Duke leaned forward. His lips brushed hers.

Then he pressed his forehead lightly into hers as he lingered close, some invisible force connecting them and drawing them together.

The soft kiss wasn't what Andi had expected. She'd always imagined their first kiss to be full of pent-up passion.

But the kiss was perfect—especially considering everything that had just happened.

Before they could talk—or kiss—anymore, the rest of the gang flooded into the room with balloons and flowers.

Duke pulled away, and they exchanged a smile.

They'd have plenty of time for kisses later.

Right now, the team needed an update.

fifty-six

THAT NIGHT, Duke took Andi home to her apartment.

He could tell she was tired—as she should be after everything she'd been through.

He hardly wanted to let her go or let her out of his sight.

But she wanted to shower, and he understood that. She insisted she would be okay, so Duke waited in the living room, listening for any signs that something could be wrong.

But mostly, he felt grateful.

Things could have turned out so much differently.

But by God's grace they hadn't.

Just as the water in the shower came on, a knock sounded at the door.

He reached for his gun.

More trouble?

He couldn't afford to let down his guard.

Cautiously, he walked toward the door and peered out the peephole.

His breath caught.

Celeste stood there, staring at the peephole as if she knew he was on the other side.

The police were searching for her.

Yet here she was.

Somehow, he wasn't surprised.

He slowly opened the door and soaked her in.

She was still as beautiful as always. But there was something new and hardened about her as well as a distance. A wall between them, almost as if they'd never been close. As if they'd never known each other.

"Are you alone?" Duke glanced behind her.

She nodded. "Can we talk?"

He looked back at the bathroom. Heard the shower still running. Knew Andi was okay.

He briefly considered calling the police. Letting them know she was here.

But he wouldn't do that. Not yet.

Then he opened the door wider. "Come in. For a minute."

She stepped inside, but Duke didn't offer a seat. Instead, the two of them stood there facing each other, a new awkwardness between them.

Celeste—that was how he'd always think of her—

swallowed hard before rubbing her palms across her jeans at her hips. "Part of me doesn't know what to say."

Duke did. "I waited for you. For two years. Searching. Praying. Agonizing."

She nodded, regret filling her gaze. "I do know that."

"Was anything real?"

"I did have a deep affection for you. But I'm not sure how many of my actions were by my choice."

He wanted to argue with her, but he couldn't, especially knowing what he did now. In many ways, she was as much of a victim as he was. But he'd need more time to fully grasp that.

"What about being here right now?" He stared at her, not giving her the chance to lie to him. "How do I know this isn't part of some other plot?"

"Because Alpine was just arrested, and the whole company was shut down. He can't control me anymore."

"Everything—all your actions—were being controlled remotely? Is that right?" He was still trying to understand the implications of these brain implants.

She nodded. "That's right. The implant is like a computer interface. Wonderful things truly can be done using this technology. But also horrible things. Usually, a person's brain transmits things to a computer, which is wonderful for someone with physical limitations. But they discovered the technology could also be reversed and impulses could be sent to a person's brain that changed their thoughts and actions."

"Was that Alpine's plan?"

"I believe it was an accident that occurred during the trial period," she said. "I think Alpine realized what a powerful tool it could be. That was when he got others on board with him. I'm hoping to have surgery to remove the implant."

"I hope that for you also." He listened and still heard the water running in the shower.

She shifted and rubbed her hands against her jeans again. "I wanted to talk to you before I turn myself in."

Duke continued to eye her, more questions simmering in his mind. "How do you know about Alpine being arrested?"

"One of my contacts told me."

Her contacts? How many people was Celeste working with?

Duke didn't like the thought. But clearly this was more than a one- or two-person operation. He expected to hear about more arrests soon.

He swallowed hard before asking, "And William? Who was he?"

"He was my handler, of sorts. But we are truly in love." She paused, hesitantly drawing her gaze up to meet his. "I'm sorry."

Duke didn't respond. What could he say?

Instead, he asked, "Did you kill James Parsons at the hospital?"

Her gaze clouded with both emotion and moisture.

She ran a finger beneath her eyes. "I'm not sure. It's all blank. But if I did, it wasn't because I wanted to. I didn't want to do any of this."

Duke nodded slowly, sensing she was telling him the truth. She was a victim also, he reminded himself. None of this had been the narrative he'd heard in his mind.

He still had more questions that he needed answers to. "Did you take those files from the CID?"

Guilt flooded her gaze. "I don't remember doing it. But I think so."

"I see." At least she wasn't denying it.

He'd simply been a pawn in all this.

And so had Celeste.

She swallowed hard, her voice becoming raspy. "I'm sorry I left you in limbo."

"You could have just broken up with me after you had what you needed."

"It was like a switch flipped in my brain. All I knew was that I needed to run. The sooner, the better." She shrugged. "I know it doesn't make sense. It doesn't make sense to me either."

"Were you and William together, even before the two of us met?"

She nodded. "I met him in Nebraska. He . . . well, he started out working for Alpine as my handler. His cover was working as a professor also. The two of us . . . we fell in love. Then I met you, and I realized I had to come to Fairbanks. He came with me."

Heat traveled up his spine and filled his cheeks.

None of what they'd had had been real. That confirmed it.

"I had glimpses of memories that flooded back to me at times . . ." Her voice cracked. "It's hard to explain. But I had these moments where I felt like myself. That was when I tried to warn you and Andi to stay away. Then the thoughts would disappear, and I almost felt like a robot."

He tried to keep his thoughts focused on answers instead of his emotions—a challenge, to say the least. But he pushed ahead.

"Were you the one who called Andi a couple of days ago?" he asked.

She shook her head. "No, I wasn't. Not to my recollection. It may have been an attempt by someone calling the shots to mess with your head. I can't say for sure."

Duke stared at Celeste another moment.

Studied the tears pooling in her gaze.

The visible tautness of her neck and shoulders.

The hesitancy marring her actions.

Part of him wanted to chew her out. But he couldn't. Not knowing what he did now.

She studied him a moment, a thoughtful look in her gaze. "I can see the way you look at Andi. I know you care about her."

"I do."

"I'm glad you found someone."

"I wish everything didn't play out the way it did,"

Duke said. "But I have to believe that everything happens for a purpose. I might not have ever met Andi if all of this hadn't happened. And I'm grateful she's been in my life."

"Seems like she's good for you."

Her image flashed through his mind, filling his chest with warmth. He slowly nodded. "She is. She really is."

———

ANDI TURNED off the water and toweled herself dry.

As she did, voices drifted from her apartment.

She froze, fear rippling through her. Had something else happened? Had one of Victor's men showed up here?

She held her breath, listening for another moment.

It was a woman, she realized.

Duke was talking to a woman.

Quietly, she cracked the door open.

Through the small opening, she spotted Duke talking to . . . Celeste.

Her breath caught.

Celeste was here?

Without the police?

As she struggled to put things together, the last part of their conversation drifted toward her.

"But I can see the way you look at Andi," Celeste said. *"I know you care about her."*

"I do."

"I'm glad you found someone. I'm sorry I left you in limbo."

"I wish everything didn't play out the way it did," Duke said. "But I have to believe that everything happens for a purpose. I might not have ever met Andi if all of this hadn't happened. And I'm grateful she's been in my life."

"Seems like she's good for you."

"She is. She really is."

His words filled Andi's chest cavity with a gooey warmth. She felt the same way.

It had been a long journey to get to this point. But she hoped to leave all that behind them as they moved forward.

She grabbed her cell phone from the bathroom counter where she'd left it.

Then she texted Gibson to let him know Celeste was here.

Maybe she shouldn't have done it. But Celeste needed to be questioned. They all needed closure. And if Celeste remained on the run . . . they'd never get that closure.

Gibson promised her he was on his way.

Then Andi threw her clothes on and stepped out, ignoring her dripping-wet hair that dampened her shirt.

Celeste looked up, not appearing surprised. To her credit, she didn't run away either.

Andi had her own questions for the woman.

"How is Victor Goodman involved with this?" Andi got right to the point.

Celeste frowned. "I don't know everything, only parts of it. I know Victor wanted to use Alpine's technology. At first, Alpine was interested in working with him. Then Alpine got greedy, and the two of them had a falling out."

"And now?" Andi asked.

She drew in a deep breath and shrugged. "Now . . . I'm not sure. But I heard the two of them had started talking again. Maybe even working together, though I doubt you could ever prove that."

Andi doubted that also. But at least things were making more sense now.

Of course, Victor would love to get his hands on technology like this. If he could control the right people . . . then nothing would stand in his way.

Even more determination hardened inside her.

Andi *would* bring Victor down. Nothing was going to stop her.

fifty-seven
A Week Later

ANDI SAT in her car outside Victor Goodman's office in Fairbanks.

Duke climbed into the car beside her and handed her some coffee.

He was going to take a shift with her. They would watch everyone coming and going from the building. Record the faces. The actions. Look for key figures.

Find answers.

Now that everything with Celeste had been resolved, for lack of a better word, Andi was giving all her attention to Victor.

Well, to Victor *and* Duke.

She reached over and squeezed Duke's hand. As she did, he leaned closer and planted a soft kiss on her cheek.

Tingles traveled from her face all the way down to her toes.

As they did every time Duke was close.

"Anything yet?" He glanced at the building.

She took a sip of her coffee. "No. That man hasn't been back."

The man she was referring to was the guy she'd seen meeting with Victor. The one who had been beaten up by those thugs—thugs who had been hired by Alpine.

Those boxes in the van? They'd been found inside the old psych building.

Not only were there implants in the tubs, as well as cash that had been paid out for jobs and weapons . . . but that picture she'd seen of James Parsons? It was just the start of it.

Dossiers had been written up for all the victims—and potential victims.

Including Andi.

It had been especially unnerving when Gibson had told her about her own photo being found there.

Things could have turned out much differently, and she thanked God for another chance, for giving her a little more time on earth.

The name of the man who'd been beaten up that night was Joe Windsor, a businessman from Texas.

Why a businessman from Texas would meet with Victor and then meet with those thugs was beyond her.

Or perhaps the possibility for the truth was more than Andi wanted to imagine.

But she was determined to get to the bottom of it.

"How did it go with Celeste?" Andi's gaze remained on the building.

She and Duke had decided that Celeste wouldn't be a taboo topic. The investigation into what she had done—or been forced to do—was ongoing.

When she and Duke had talked earlier, Andi had given her blessing on the idea of keeping an open dialogue about everything. The more answers Duke had, the more closure he would eventually have.

She would never want to take that from him.

For that reason, Duke had met twice with Celeste at the jail where she was being held.

"Celeste has been putting together bits and pieces of what happened," Duke started. "Apparently, she *did* work for Compassion Mission. Everything was hush-hush as Alpine tried to get the organization off the ground. At first, it had seemed like a dream job to her. She loved what they were doing. Loved helping people who couldn't help themselves."

"Then what happened?"

"Celeste noticed some debatable things going on within the company, and she started asking questions. The more questions she asked, the more danger she put herself in. A doctor down in California actually headed the program, and he had a woman he was training under him—someone everyone called Nurse Reaper."

"Are Nurse Reaper and Nursy Mercy the same person?"

"No, not really. Nurse Reaper was training Celeste to eventually take over her job. I'm sure there were more people involved. But the original doctor and Nurse Reaper have been arrested, as I'm sure you've heard on the news. This doctor apparently asked Celeste to meet one night, to stay after so they could talk about her concerns. But it was all a trap."

A trap? Memories of being tied down to that operating table began to pummel Andi, and she squeezed her eyes shut. A shiver raked through her as she remembered the terror she'd experienced.

Things could have ended so differently . . .

"Apparently, Celeste knew something was wrong, and she tried to get away," Duke continued. "But the doctor caught her and put her under. The next thing she remembered, she was awake and compliant, almost as if nothing had happened. But she knew something had changed."

"Then from there, someone—I'm assuming someone Alpine hired—began to train her so Alpine could eventually use her as a pawn," Andi finished, her lips tugging down in a frown. "He told her what to do. Who to kill. Where to move. I'm surprised he got away with it for this long."

"He and his team were good at what they were doing." Duke's voice tightened. "They knew how to cover their tracks. Knew what medications to use that wouldn't be looked for in an autopsy. They chose the people they helped very carefully. People who didn't have a strong family to raise concerns or put up a fuss."

"Did she mention the Craig connection?"

"She said Craig came around asking questions. On her way to Gates of the Arctic, she stopped by his place to 'talk.' It got heated, and her bracelet broke off. She said she had no choice but to flee. Craig must have died before he could pursue the truth anymore."

Andi turned away from the building, needing to see Duke's face.

She skimmed her fingers over his jaw, loving how she had the freedom to do so now. Loving that the walls between them had finally come down.

"I'm sorry you had to go through everything you did to get these answers." Her voice lilted softly. "But I'm glad this program was shut down."

His gaze latched onto hers. "Me too."

"What about William?"

"He's awake. He's still standing by Celeste and is basically backing up her story. But, considering his involvement in everything, it wouldn't surprise me if he's arrested as soon as he's medically able to leave the hospital."

Andi supposed that was good news that William was okay. He could also provide more answers. It seemed as if Celeste truly did care about the man. She'd need someone there for her as she processed everything that had happened to her.

Andi let her hand drift from Duke's cheek until it

rested on his chest. "Another thing that doesn't make sense—why in the world did Celeste and William stay in Fairbanks, even after she was supposed to leave you and disappear?"

"I asked her that. She said Fairbanks seemed like the safest place to stay, somewhere I wouldn't think to look for them. I wasn't expecting her to show up here. I was looking at Gates of the Artic and the surrounding area. Ranger confirmed that Celeste *did* go to the park. But Celeste doesn't remember much from that time or what happened."

"Right." That made sense, given the rest of her story.

"Afterward, Celeste basically stayed inside while William went to work. When we showed up at their house that day, they panicked. Alpine hired some men and moved them out that night before we could go back and find them. He didn't want us to ruin their plan."

"This sounds like something straight out of a sci-fi novel at times, doesn't it?"

Duke released a dry laugh. "You can say that again. I never thought this might actually be reality."

"None of us did."

"Celeste really did have that implant," Duke said. "Her surgery to remove it was yesterday, so she's still trying to adjust to having free will again. The feds believe she truly did kill James Parsons as well as those other patients at the hospital. She'll definitely be going to trial."

Andi crossed her arms. That was the first she'd heard that update. "That will be an interesting trial. Sure, Celeste may have physically committed the crimes, but mentally . . . she was being controlled. I can't say there's ever been another case like that before. It almost makes me want to get my law license again and offer to represent her."

Duke raised his eyebrows. "You've thought about getting your law license again?"

She shrugged. "I don't know. Maybe. I mean, part of me is intrigued by the idea. I can't keep doing what I'm doing forever."

Those words were the truth. She supposed she'd given the idea a thought or two on occasion. But nothing too serious.

She had other matters she wanted to consider first.

Updates had been trickling in all week.

Test results had come back on Simmy and Mariella. They were the only ones who had eaten some of the pastries set out by Alfonso. But apparently those pastries had been tampered with using some kind of drug that induced nausea.

Evelyn had been responsible. Might have even been responsible for Mariella's tires being slashed, although Kyle could have also done that. At this point, it didn't really matter. The two of them were in this together.

Evelyn was also a part of Alpine's program through Compassion Mission. She had somehow sneaked into the lodge and placed the poison in the food, hoping to take the whole team out.

But that hadn't happened.

Apparently, she had also been watching them, along with Kyle.

Alpine had put so many steps in place to ensure the murder club didn't get too close to finding out the actual truth.

When he'd learned Duke was still investigating Celeste's disappearance, and that he now had a team of podcasters helping him, he'd known he needed to act—and taking out all six of them would have been suspicious. So he'd done the next best thing.

He'd hired them. Doing so allowed him to keep them in his pocket, so he could know what was going on with them and control some of the narrative. Duke being involved with the group was the icing on the cake.

Since Alpine's arrest, his face and name had been splashed all over the news. In fact, that was all reporters wanted to talk about. How the mighty had fallen.

The truth was, if Alpine had succeeded in perfecting this technology, Andi could only imagine the ways it could be used to harm others.

That was probably where Victor came in. He wanted to get his hands on that technology so he could manipulate people into doing things he wanted.

She had no doubt about that.

However, Alpine had been tight-lipped concerning

the business mogul. From everything she'd learned, Alpine had never once even mentioned Victor's name.

There had been no articles about his arrest.

Not yet.

Andi was determined to change that.

She'd make sure everyone knew what Victor Goodman was guilty of.

But how far would Victor go to keep her quiet?

He was becoming desperate.

That made her nervous—not for herself, but for her friends.

For Duke.

What if one of them got hurt because of her investigation?

She wouldn't be able to forgive herself.

But she'd come too far to give up now.

Victor Goodman would be stopped once and for all.

She turned back to the building she was watching.

Andi would make sure that man got justice, even if it was the last thing she did.

~~~

Thank you for reading The Secrets She Kept. If you enjoyed this book, please consider leaving a review.

The exciting conclusion of the True Crime Junkies series is coming soon.
~~~

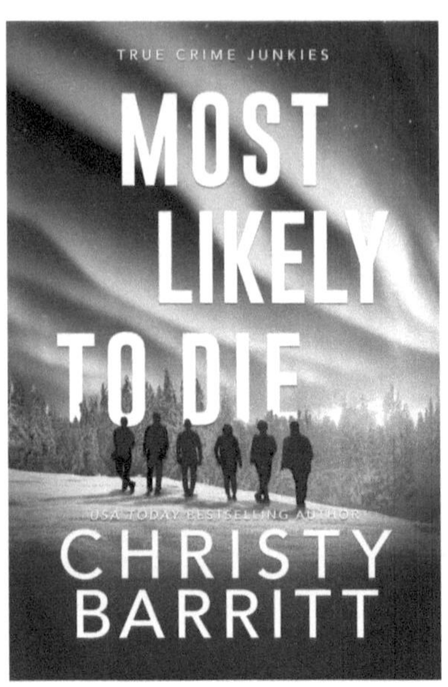

TRUE CRIME JUNKIES
MOST
LIKELY
TO DIE
USA TODAY BESTSELLING AUTHOR
CHRISTY
BARRITT

complete book list

Squeaky Clean Mysteries
#1 Hazardous Duty
Half Witted (Squeaky Clean In Between Mysteries Book 1, novella)
#2 Suspicious Minds
#2.5 It Came Upon a Midnight Crime (novella)
Half Truth (Squeaky Clean In Between Mysteries Book 2, novella)
#3 Organized Grime
#4 Dirty Deeds
#5 The Scum of All Fears
#6 To Love, Honor and Perish
#7 Mucky Streak
#8 Foul Play
#9 Broom & Gloom
#10 Dust and Obey

#11 Thrill Squeaker
#11.5 Swept Away (novella)
#12 Cunning Attractions
#13 Cold Case: Clean Getaway
#14 Cold Case: Clean Sweep
#15 Cold Case: Clean Break
#16 Cleans to an End
While You Were Sweeping, A Riley Thomas Spinoff

The Sierra Files

#1 Pounced
#2 Hunted
#3 Pranced
#4 Rattled

Lantern Beach Mysteries

#1 Hidden Currents
#2 Flood Watch
#3 Storm Surge
#4 Dangerous Waters
#5 Perilous Riptide
#6 Deadly Undertow

Lantern Beach Romantic Suspense

#1 Tides of Deception
#2 Shadow of Intrigue
#3 Storm of Doubt
#4 Winds of Danger

#5 Rains of Remorse
#6 Torrents of Fear

Lantern Beach P.D.

#1 On the Lookout
#2 Attempt to Locate
#3 First Degree Murder
#4 Dead on Arrival
#5 Plan of Action

Lantern Beach Escape

Afterglow (a novelette)

Lantern Beach Blackout

#1 Dark Water
#2 Safe Harbor
#3 Ripple Effect
#4 Rising Tide

Lantern Beach Guardians

#1 Hide and Seek
#2 Shock and Awe
#3 Safe and Sound

Lantern Beach Blackout: The New Recruits

#1 Rocco
#2 Axel
#3 Beckett

#4 Gabe

Lantern Beach Mayday
#1 Run Aground
#2 Dead Reckoning
#3 Tipping Point

Lantern Beach Christmas
Silent Night

Lantern Beach Blackout: Danger Rising
#1 Brandon
#2 Dylan
#3 Maddox
#4 Titus

Beach Bound Books and Beans Mysteries
#1 Bound by Murder
#2 Bound by Disaster
#3 Bound by Mystery
#4 Bound by Trouble
#5 Bound by Mayhem

Lantern Beach Exposure
#1 Fractured Lies
#2 Shattered Whispers
#3 Unsteady Ground
#4 Troubled Graves

#5 Deceptive Shallows
#6 Secret Shores

True Crime Junkies
#1 Just the Nicest Person
#2 He Walks Among Us
#3 Never Happen to You
#4 The Dead of Night
#5 Leave the Lights On
#6 The End of the Road
#7 The Secrets She Kept
#8 Most Likely to Die

The Shadow Agency
#1 Shadow Operative
#2 Shadow Chaser

Fog Lake Suspense
#1 Edge of Peril
#2 Margin of Error
#3 Brink of Danger
#4 Line of Duty
#5 Legacy of Lies
#6 Secrets of Shame
#7 Refuge of Redemption

Vanishing Ranch
#1 Forgotten Secrets

#2 Necessary Risk
#3 Risky Ambition
#4 Deadly Intent
#5 Lethal Betrayal
#6 High Stakes Deception
#7 Fatal Vendetta
#8 Troubled Tidings
#9 Narrow Escape
#10 Desperate Rescue

Saltwater Cowboys
#1 Saltwater Cowboy
#2 Breakwater Protector
#3 Cape Corral Keeper
#4 Seagrass Secrets
#5 Driftwood Danger
#6 Unwavering Security

Beach House Mysteries
#1 The Cottage on Ghost Lane
#2 The Inn on Hanging Hill
#3 The House on Dagger Point
#4 The Bungalow on Shadow Road

The Worst Detective Ever
#1 Ready to Fumble
#2 Reign of Error
#3 Safety in Blunders

#4 Join the Flub

#5 Blooper Freak

Raven Remington Relentless

#6 Flaw Abiding Citizen

#7 Gaffe Out Loud

#8 Joke and Dagger

#9 Wreck the Halls

#10 Glitch and Famous

#11 Not on My Botch

#12 One Hit Blunder

Holly Anna Paladin Mysteries

#1 Random Acts of Murder

#2 Random Acts of Deceit

#2.5 Random Acts of Scrooge

#3 Random Acts of Malice

#4 Random Acts of Greed

#5 Random Acts of Fraud

#6 Random Acts of Outrage

#7 Random Acts of Iniquity

Cape Thomas Series

#1 Dubiosity

#2 Disillusioned

#3 Distorted

Carolina Moon Series

#1 Home Before Dark

#2 Gone By Dark
#3 Wait Until Dark
#4 Light the Dark
#5 Taken By Dark

The Sidekick's Survival Guide

#1 The Art of Eavesdropping
#2 The Perks of Meddling
#3 The Exercise of Interfering
#4 The Practice of Prying
#5 The Skill of Snooping
#6 The Craft of Being Covert

School of Hard Rocks Mysteries

#1 The Treble with Murder
#2 Crime Strikes a Chord
#3 Tone Death

Standalone Romantic Suspense

Keeping Guard
The Last Target
Race Against Time
Ricochet
Key Witness
Lifeline
High-Stakes Holiday Reunion
Desperate Measures
Hidden Agenda

Mountain Hideaway
Dark Harbor
Shadow of Suspicion
The Baby Assignment
The Cradle Conspiracy
Trained to Defend
Mountain Survival
Dangerous Mountain Rescue
Lethal Mountain Pursuit

Crime á la Mode Mysteries
#1 Dead Man's Float
#2 Milkshake Up
#3 Bomb Pop Threat
#4 Banana Split Personalities

Standalone Novels
Death of the Couch Potato's Wife
Imperfect
The Good Girl
The Wrecking

Standalone Sweet Christmas Novellas
Home to Chestnut Grove
How Her Ex Stole Christmas

The Gabby St. Claire Diaries (a Tween Mystery series)

#1 The Curtain Call Caper
#2 The Disappearing Dog Dilemma
#3 The Bungled Bike Burglaries

Nonfiction

Characters in the Kitchen

Changed: True Stories of Finding God through Christian Music (out of print)

The Novel in Me: The Beginner's Guide to Writing and Publishing a Novel (out of print)

about the author

USA Today has called Christy Barritt's books "scary, funny, passionate, and quirky."

Christy writes both mystery and romantic suspense novels that are clean with underlying messages of faith. Her books have sold more than four million copies and have won the Daphne du Maurier Award for Excellence in Suspense and Mystery, have been twice nominated for the Romantic Times Reviewers' Choice Award, and have finaled for both a Carol Award and Foreword Magazine's Book of the Year.

She is married to her Prince Charming, a man who thinks she's hilarious—but only when she's not trying to be. Christy is a self-proclaimed klutz, an avid music lover who's known for spontaneously bursting into song, and a road trip aficionado.

When she's not working or spending time with her family, she enjoys singing, playing the guitar, and exploring small, unsuspecting towns where people have no idea how accident-prone she is.

Find Christy online at: **www.christybarritt.com**

Sign up for Christy's newsletter to get information on all of her latest releases here: **www.christybarritt.com/newsletter-sign-up/**

facebook.com/AuthorChristyBarritt

x.com/christybarritt

instagram.com/cebarritt